1

100

FUNNY SHORT STORIES
FOR SENIORS AND THE ELDERLY

*Funny and Inspiring Short Novels and
Essays to Stimulate the Mind*

Crazy Trivia Stories for Adults Series

Christian Stahl

First published in Great Britain in 2023 by Midealuck Publishing Ltd.

The right of Christian Stahl to be identified as the Author of the work has been asserted by him in accordance with the Copyright.

ISBN 9781739249175

Table of Contents

Chapter I

Short Novels Based on a True Story
Seniors Make the World Go Round

Mr. Dementia

Experience teaches us that the world is not a nursery

- Plato

According to the nurses, I turned 82 today.

Even though most of them are as helpful as lumps in the lungs, I believe them. So, for this birthday, which is nothing to be sneezed at, I wanted to plan something special for my "colleagues" — my housemates here in the nursing home.

Inevitably, the nurses intervened. Catching wind of my good intentions, they demanded a discussion with management. And according to big nurse Berta, it could take a while.

I don't have much to do here, so I've spent most of my time taking care of others. Often going as far as giving small gifts to the old-timers here in the nursing home.

You only turn 82 once, so I plan to give the staff a few presents again; old photos, postcards, and trinkets, things I've been allowed to collect and keep over the years.

Once, I gave big Berta, our chief warden, as I call her, three 1960s Florida beach postcards in pristine condition.

And Jimmy, the young dim-witted orderly, I recently gave him a Georgia beach postcard.

I also gave the two sisters responsible for my hygiene two mixed old postcards each.

I was advised to keep an inventory record of my collections and belongings because I apparently suffer from dementia. Fuck them! Yes, you heard right — I don't give a damn what they say.

Do I sound somewhat bitter? Some of the residents would say I'm evil, but the nurses understand my behavior is due to dementia.

Most other folks though, are cheerful and content most of the time — and you can say I'm somewhat responsible for that.

Oh, I almost forgot — An excellent example was on another birthday. Not only did I gift postcards, but I also went the extra mile for everyone and hired a live band.

And as big Berta likes to remind me, even hired an external catering service with yes sir... steak and lobster!

Admittedly, alcohol is forbidden here, but not on that occasion —not on my birthday. So, I paid for it to be secretly provided.

Am I rich? Possibly, who knows? But where did the money come from while living as a nursing home resident? Well, let me start at the beginning. As I've said, I'm known to suffer from dementia.

A year or two ago, I still lived independently in a rough neighborhood in central Detroit.

I had been living there since 1961. But before that, if memory serves, I lived a block away with my mother until she passed. I never did marry, and to this day, I remain single.

Anyway, I was punctual in paying my rent and never defaulted on any bills. Back then, every apartment in the area was home to a small family, but, over the years, the neighborhood deteriorated. One after another, neighbors moved out.

And what began moving in were some rather strange characters. Immigrants, gangs, and complete strangers, to name a few. But, at any rate, I didn't care, and I wasn't afraid. So, I stood my ground and stayed put.

I saw cliques of teens hanging around old cars and trucks, making deals daily. Admittedly, crime was on the rise, but somehow, it never worried me. I kept to myself and stayed out of trouble, becoming a familiar fixture, almost invincible to those around me.

They likely heard or assumed I was a bit absentminded, having regularly witnessed me locking myself out of my apartment on numerous occasions.

One day, while looking out the window, I heard screaming and shouting. I leant out to look, and what a scene it was!

Three young Hispanic-looking guys were chasing a black man.

Suddenly, I heard gunshots! I slammed the window shut and willed myself to forget about the incident.

Later that day, the police knocked on my door, inquiring if I had seen or heard anything.

Of course, I denied seeing anything, but the cop insisted that I must have noticed something because the incident occurred right outside my apartment. Casually mentioning that I suffered from dementia, I insistently denied memory of any incident.

The following morning, I ran into one of the neighbors in the stairwell—a youngish looking guy.

"Hey, Gramps," he said, "I overheard the cops asking you questions, and you gave them nothing. I appreciate that."

"Sure thing," I said.

"Wait a minute... oh man, you're Herby, right? I heard you've been living here since around the fifties?"

"Something like that," I said.

We had a bit of a chat, joked around and instantly hit it off.

Over the following months, we continued building a friendship and began referring to them as my grandson and his other cousins.

Eventually, my new friend, Cesar, invited me to his family home in a different neighborhood. Let me tell you, they were living it up with high-class parties. It was clear these folks were not poverty-stricken. In fact, it was at one of those parties where I got the steak and lobster delivery idea. As it happened, I became part of their inner circle, or part of their club, as they say.

One day Cesar asked me if I could deliver a small package to a car parked in a lot just two blocks away.

Sure I could. Long story short, we made some money, and I was happy to be earning extra cash in addition to my disability pension.

I felt free again. About a year later, the doctor that regularly visited to check on my "mental condition" informed me that I could no longer live unsupervised.

At eighty years old, I was not allowed to live alone anymore!

Of course, this whole situation developed into quite a scene with my new family friends who intended to keep me home.

Ultimately, the bureaucrats, doctors and even the cops all worked together. Twelve times they came to my home with doctors, advisors, and experts, but I believe that that stupid cop from last year finally made it happen. Though the truth is, I was conceding that, at some point, I needed to go into a nursing home. It didn't help that my friends insisted that I stay — I had to go. It was the unhappiest moment in my life. However, before we said goodbye, we made a "pact".

The beginning here was hard, of course. I had to adapt to this place, but I kept in touch with everyone. The secret is that I started small. I had a small side hustle going on right here in this institution.

Every week Cesar sent a bag with pink pills, deeply discounted, which allowed for an impressive profit.

What did I do with those pills? After convincing them of the pills' power to improve their energy and mood, I gave them to my new resident neighbors.

They loved my stuff more than Jell-O and their grandchildren combined. It was the greatest invention since sliced bread for them.

Of course, it cost them, particularly the older ones with limited mobility who needed more. But they were happy to pay because, truthfully, the medication breathed new life into them, giving some of them a reason to live again. So, as you can imagine, the orders grew, and over time, business boomed.

Some of the staff here became suspicious that I was up to something.

To get them off my back and keep them quiet, I bribed them with cash, starting small and going from there.

So, everyone scored, and everyone was happy. Well, almost everyone. Those who didn't pay timely received a not-so-friendly visit from a few of my non-English speaking relatives.

Boy, do we have fun in here sometimes! And do I have dementia? Dementia, my ass!

The Tiger

Based on a True Story

Despite the wedding day, Berta and Jimmy just sat in the room with a cup of instant coffee and chocolate cookies. The reason for this meager celebration was that they were living in a nursing home. Neither particularly happy nor unhappy, because at least, they were given the opportunity to live in a room. A bright spot of their life was the beautiful view, because the retirement home was in a high-rise building, on the 10th floor. And the couple enjoyed the view, because that was about all they had left in life.

"The view still fascinates me Jimmy, isn't it beautiful here?"

Jimmy puts on his glasses. "I can see the sky," Jimmy says in a raspy voice. "But still, we always look at the same skyscraper across the street."

"Yeah that's right Jimmy." Berta adjusts her glasses. "But otherwise, they have nice windows back there."

Jimmy shakes his head slightly. "That evil tiger is driving me crazy."

"Jimmy?"

"The tiger peeking out the window there. From the building across the street, on the 8th floor."

"A tiger? There aren't any tigers around here, are there?"

"Oh yes there are, right there" Jimmy points with trembling fingers to a window opposite.

Berta rises. "Jimmy, I see a big head of an animal! Right there!"

"Yes, yes, that's the one. That's a full grown tiger standing up on its hind legs and looking out the window."

"But how is that possible Jimmy? A tiger, here in Brooklyn?"

"That shouldn't be possible! You know what, I'll check with the staff here, maybe they know something."
It came as it had to come. Old Eddy, the corpulent head supervisor listens patiently to Jimmy's story. Finally, in a soothing voice, he says with a slight smile. "What can I tell you, this is America and there are no tigers here."

"Listen to us," says Berta slightly agitated. "I have seen the animal too."

"Come on folks, let's all get back to the room. No tigers in Brooklyn, okay now."

The couple gets up, at the door Berta turns around. "You should take this seriously before something bad happens."

In the following weeks, Berta and Jimmy see the tiger more often, irregularly, but for them it is a fact that this tiger is no imagination or dementia. In fact, they have become accustomed to the tiger looking out of the window, and especially Berta has taken the tiger to her heart. But what use all complaints if others hold one for dementia?

One morning, when it is still dark, they hear a loud knocking at the door. Berta almost falls out of bed in her haste to get to the door, and as she briefly looks out the window, she can hardly believe what is happening down on the street. Police cars, ambulances and fire brigades everywhere. Hopefully no mass shooting, Berta hopes.

As she opens the door, she is totally perplexed to see a police officer accompanied by the nursing home manager. "Miss Jones," the polite officer asks half-smiling.

"How can I help you?"

"Sorry to bother you so early, but we need you as a witness."

"For what?"

"Actually, you and your husband?"

The supervisor Eddy interrupts. "You saw the tiger from your room, didn't you?"

"The tiger? Sure, what about him?"

"Well, we need you to be a witness that there was a tiger living across the street in the apartment."

Berta's eyes widened "was...?"
The officer, "so it's true then. You know, a young man has had a tiger in the apartment across the street, and this morning the tiger escaped."

"Did the cat go back to the apartment?"

"Sorry Mam, but we had to destroy the animal."

At that moment Berta becomes dizzy, she rolls her eyes and falls over. At the last moment Jimmy is able to catch her. He scolds Eddy. "See, we were right. If only you had listened to us old folks...."

The officer turns to the supervisor. "He's right ...because if we listened more to the elders, not only would animal lives be saved but millions of people as well."

Our Counseling Session

Karen and her husband Toni went for counseling after 30 years of marriage. When asked what the problem was, Karen went into a passionate, painful tirade listing every problem they had ever had in the 30 years they had been married. She went on and on and on: neglect, lack of intimacy, emptiness, loneliness, feeling unloved and unlovable, an entire laundry list of unmet needs she had endured over the course of their marriage. Finally, after allowing this to go for a sufficient length of time, the therapist got up, walked around the desk and after asking Karen to stand, embraced her, unbuttoned her blouse and bra. Put his hand on her breasts and massaged them thoroughly, while kissing her passionately as her husband Toni watched with raised eyebrow! Karen shut up, buttoned up her blouse, and quietly sat down while basking in the glow of being highly aroused. The therapist turned to Toni and said, "this is what your wife needs at least three times a week. Can you do this?"

Toni thought for a moment and replied, "well, I can drop off here on Mondays and Wednesdays, but on Fridays I play golf."

Chapter II

Wedding Anniversary Humor

The Confession

Bill, now in is post prosperous post middle age, was complacently celebrating his 35th wedding anniversary with Grace, enjoying a cigar and 21 year old scotch when, turning he asked: "Grace, we've been married 35 years and there's only one thing I'd like to know and that is have ever been unfaithful to me?"

"Bill" said Grace earnestly, "I have to be honest with you. Yes, I've been unfaithful on three occasions during those 35 years, but only with good reasons".
A bit taken back, Bill looked shaken but asked: "I never suspected, can you tell me what you mean by good reasons? Grace responded: "The very first time was just after we were married and we are about to lose the family farm after the drought and those bushfires, and the bank manager threatened to foreclose. I went into own that afternoon and you might remember the very next day, he drove out to tell us the loan had been extended and the interest rate shaved".

Magnanimously, Bill said "I can forgive you for that. You saved the farm and we've never looked back, but what about the second time?"

"A few years later you suffered that massive heart attack and we couldn't afford the highly expensive surgeon but, after I visited him, he not only performed the operation but did so at no fee…"

"Right, I do remember that it saved my life, so of course I can forgive you for that. But now we're well off, what about the third occasion?"

"Yes", Grace smiled with a far-off look in her eye. "We were quite well off but do you remember when you first ran for president of the golf club…..And you needed 73 more votes?"

Men do Remember Anniversaries

A woman awakes during the night to find that her husband was not in their bed. She put on her dressing gown and goes downstairs to look for him. She finds him sitting at the kitchen table with a hot cup of coffee in front of him. He appears to be in deep thought, just starring at the wall. She watches as he wipes a tear from his eyes and take sip of his coffee!

"What's the matter dear?" She whispers as he steps into the room. Why are you down here at this time of night? The husband looks up from his coffee. "I am just remembering when we first met 20 years ago and started dating. You were only 16. Do you remember back then?....he says solemnly. The wife is touched to tears thinking that her husband is so caring , so sensitive. "Yes, of course honey…" she replies.

The husband pauses. The words were not coming easily. "Do you remember when your father caught us in the backseat of my car?"

"Yes, I remember" the wife says, lowering herself into a chair beside him.

The husband continuous. "Do you remember when he shoved a shotgun in my face and said: "Either you marry my daughter, or I will send you to jail for 20 years?"

"I remember that too", she replies softly. He wipes another tear from his cheek and says…"I would have been released today…."

A Successful Marriage

Bill and Alice were celebrating 60 years of marriage. When a friend asked Bill for the secret to their long, successful marriage, Bill replied, "We have always taken the time to go to a lovely restaurant twice a week. Good food, a little candlelight, fine wine, soft music and some dancing. "

"That's wonderful," said the friend.

Bill retorted, "Yes, I go Wednesdays and she goes Fridays."

The Secret

My Grandparents were celebrating 75 years of marriage, so I asked Grandpa what the secret to a long-lasting union was. He replied, "Two things, buddy: Number one is whenever you are wrong, admit it. Secondly, whenever you are right, say nothing."

A Proposal in a Special Place

Maggie and George have been sitting across from each other over coffee and cookies for over an hour. Although today is their 30th wedding anniversary, they actually don't have much to say to each other. After another 30 minutes, Maggie has had enough. She snaps at him angrily.

"Come on talk to me, you are not suffering from dementia!"

Slowly George raises his head. "I believe you, and I know it's our anniversary."

"Good to know you remember George."

"I see our rings, but I just cannot remember where we got married."

Maggie shakes her head. "Well, I hope you remember at least where you're proposing me."

George scratches his chin. "It was in a coffee shop."

"No George, actually it was a bar."

"A bar?"

"A bar, it was a bar for special occasions."

Harry scratches his head. "If that's so… a very long occasion I suppose."

"Honey, actually it was a short time bar …or sort of."

"No, I can't believe it …and as you know, I was never a drinker."

Maggi winks at him, then holds his hand with both hands. "I know that honey."

"love you, but this story with that bar I really don't remember, " says Harry shaking his head.

"Don't you remember, it was our first kiss in there."

"You kissed me?" Harry buries his hands in his face.

"Of course, and you wanted to kiss properly too."

Harry stares at her in horror. "How many, you know, did you put in your mouth that night?"

Maggie's eyes darken. "Now don't be vulgar Harry, stop it!"

"You are right," he said and nods timidly. Wearily he reaches across, holds her hand for a second, and tries to get back to sleep.

A few moments later she says. "Then you really use to kiss me."

Mildly irritated he reaches across, gives her a peck on the cheek, and settles down to sleep again.

Thirty seconds later she says, "Then you use to bite my neck."

Angrily he gets up, hisses at her some inaudible words and stumbles towards to bathroom.

"Why are so serious honey, where are you going?"

To get my set of teeth and to annul our marriage once and for all.

Her Part

Bert and Marge had been married for 60 years and they still held hands whenever they went out. When Bert was asked about this, his reply was simple. "When I let go, she's off shopping."

The Cocktail Party

At a cocktail party, one woman said to another, "Aren't you wearing your wedding ring on the wrong finger?"
The other replies, "Yes, I am. I married the wrong man."

The Wedding Day

The bride and groom were specially driven up to the church in a vintage limousine.
The people clap as the elegantly dressed groom and the bride in beige colored wedding dress in oversize get out of the car and walk directly to the church.

Rose is distraught. This morning Paul didn't want to go right away, again they had a fight over diapers, Rose left alone, but Paul had promised to follow by cab.

Finally the crowd of people moves into the church, even the pastor holds the door open. The people take their seats, and all are full of friends, only occasional glances directed at Rosie reveal that there must have been a problem with her and her absent husband. Where was Paul? Rose began to cry, Suddenly she hears screaming, Paul's words. She runs to the entrance. With horror she sees the pastor trying to close the door and Paul pushing against the door. "Let me in asshole," He yells.

Rosie jumps up. "What's going on here? Let my husband in!" The pastor turns to Rosie, pale with anger. "Look at your husband, he's trying to get into the church like that, I can't let him!"

Rose doesn't want to know any more, and tears open the door with all her might, and old Paul storms into the church. But suddenly all is quiet, with amusement the guests observe that good old Paul is wearing a suit jacket and tie, but instead of pants had only black garbage bags tied around his legs.

"Don't stare so stupid," Paul says bitingly. "Plastic is fantastic, ...you Morons."

On the Deathbed

A very old, sick man lay dying in his bed. He felt that the end was coming soon when suddenly a wonderful smell reached him. Though he wasn't quite himself anymore, his instinct told him, "These are my favorite cookies! Anise cookies!" Gathering all the strength he had left, he got out of bed to gasp for air and run toward the delicious smell. With difficulty he took one step at a time as he stabilized himself against the wall and slowly fought his way down the stairs, step by step. Completely exhausted, but arrived on the ground floor, he leaned against the door frame and peered curiously into the bakery. He wasn't sure whether he was already in paradise or dreaming: neatly spread out on the baking paper, dozens of his beloved aniseed biscuits were ready to be eaten on the kitchen table. Or was he already with the Lord God?

But maybe it was also a final token of love from his wife, to whom he had been married for over 50 years? With a great effort he lowered himself towards the table and waited on his knees. His chapped lips parted with the euphoric prospect. Almost drooling, he already felt the dreamlike aroma of the cookies on his tongue. His aged, wrinkled hand trembled gingerly toward a spot on the corner of the table. Suddenly a soup ladle whipped his hand: "Hands off," his wife drooled, "these are for the funeral!"

The Golden Wedding Anniversary

The elderly couple celebrates their golden wedding anniversary. "Do you remember back then?" she remembers. "You were in such a hurry I didn't even have time to take off my stockings!" "Yes," says grandpa thoughtfully, "and today you have enough time to knit a pair beforehand."…..

A Special Present

Grandmother is looking for a special present for her husband on their wedding anniversary. It's not easy, because at his age he already has everything.

At the end, grandmother is standing in front of a shelf full of condoms in the department store. She thinks, *great, flavored condoms, I'll try that at home.* Grandma buys a full box of mixed flavors. As soon as she gets home she shows the purchase to her elderly but still lusty husband.

"That's fantastic! Condoms with taste, we'll test them right away."

They go right into the bedroom, close the door and turn off the lights.

Grandma: "Mmmmmmh… delicious, gorgonzola cheese…"

Grandpa: "Wait, let me put it on first!"

True Love

Says one senior to the other: "I've been married for thirty years and have spent every evening at my wife's house."

"This is true love."

"No, that's my rheumatism."

The Routine

On the occasion of his 95th birthday, an elderly man in a nursing home is interviewed for a report in the local newspaper. Reporter: "How do you feel at your age and in this environment?" Old man: "Thank you, very good." Reporter: "What's your daily routine like in here?" Old man: "In the morning: piss first." Reporter: "And? No problems?" Old man: "Oh wow. Hard beam, no burning, healthy colour." Reporter: "And then?" Old man: "Stool." Reporter: "Any complaints?" Old man: "Not a trace. Sufficient pressure, no blood, normal bowel movements." Reporter: "What's next then?" Old man: "Well, then I'll get up."

Chapter III

Seniors at Sea and Old Memories

The Haunting

The grass is still damp from the overnight rain, even now in the late morning when Mari and a few others walk slowly from the common room of the nursing home towards the pavilion. A nurse guides the small group, not one of them younger than ninety.

'Mari, maybe you'd like to share with everyone the story you told me yesterday,' says the nurse, Cleo, as she arranges the chairs.

Mari nods. 'Yes. I was thinking about it last night. There were things I forgot to tell you. Terrible things. Things I thought that I would never forget.'

'Don't scare everyone, now,' says Cleo, smiling.

'This happened when I was very young,' Mari began.

An old man walks towards them, older even than any of the people sitting in the pavilion. Hunched over with age, he almost resembles a gargoyle from a cathedral spire. Cleo pauses, offering to help, but the old man waves her away and takes a seat with the rest of the group and swivels his pale, watery blue eyes towards Mari.

'Are you new here?' one of them asks.

The old man seems to nod.

'You're so familiar,' says Mari. 'But I can't remember from where, I'm sorry. Maybe I'm forgetting faces now.'

'Tell us the story, Mari,' says one of the old men. 'Cleo says it's a good one.'

Mari nods, but her eyes don't leave the face of the stranger. 'As I was saying, this all happened a very long time ago.'

'I was on holiday, in Genoa. Bill and I had just got engaged. We didn't see much of the city. We were so happy just being together that it was enough to walk along the shore. I didn't care that we were missing out on seeing the Palazzi dei Rolli.

It became our habit to go down to the harbor and watch the sunrise, listen to the gulls and all the fishermen starting work. This morning we walked farther than usual, around to the dry docks, where the ships are repaired and built. There was one ship in particular that caught our attention. It was a new ocean liner, quite small. It was designed to take fewer passengers, but it would offer a luxury service. The design was cutting edge for the time, in particular its double-skinned hull.

I remember seeing it half-complete, hanging out of the water. Like a skeleton. There were two workmen arguing on shore. They seemed very upset. But of course they were speaking in Italian – I couldn't understand them.

Bill and I got married that summer. We didn't have any ideas about our honeymoon, but one morning Bill opened the newspaper and there was an advertisement for the ship. Its maiden voyage, from Southampton to New York. It seemed perfect.

It was extraordinary to see the boat completed. It spanned three decks, and where most cruise ships of the time were bulky, like a tall building turned on its side, this ship was sleek, almost like a superyacht, except no one had built one of them before. It was the first of its kind. It balanced on the water like a knife, and its black hull gleamed like polished marble.

Those first nights – I don't think I've ever danced so much! The band played late into the night and most of us on board were young and there to enjoy ourselves. But there was one man who wasn't having fun. He wouldn't dance, he only sat there in the corner, drinking. He was a crooked, sour-faced man. He had dark circles under his blue eyes, like he hadn't slept in weeks. His clothes were expensive, but unclean. I remember thinking he must have been a manual worker, because his hands were covered in tiny white scars. Everyone thought it best to keep away from him, but I made the mistake of talking to him one night. He claimed to have been an engineer who worked on the construction of the ship and he told me this nasty little story about punishing a worker who'd made mistakes during the ship's construction. I could smell the alcohol on his breath, so I didn't take him seriously. It just seemed like the ravings of an unpleasant drunk.

The thing is, I think part of the reason we all danced so late is that none of us wanted to go to bed. Because as soon as you went to bed all you could listen to were the sounds of the ship at night. The wind and the waves and the creaking of the hull. These were all normal sounds, but there were other things. Voices. At first I thought it must be my mind playing tricks on me, but when I finally told Bill what I heard, he said that he had heard it too. A friend we had made on board, Lucy, said maybe it was a ghost. People were much more superstitious back then, it didn't seem like a strange thing to think.

But then every night we'd get dressed up and we'd go to the ballroom, where the musicians were waiting for us in their evening suits. And the music would start and we'd get to our feet and dance and dance and forget all about the voices.

I can still remember the feeling of being out in the Atlantic, so far from everything. Nothing but the ocean for miles, dark cloud rolling across the endless sky, the gentle pitching of the ship whenever we met a wave.

A week into the voyage, the strange voices became harder to ignore. We could tell the crew members were edgy – they were hearing the voices as well. And not just voices. There were knocking sounds all over the ship, in different places every night. Like something was trying to claw through the walls.

Every night we'd keep going up to the ballroom, but no one danced anymore. Our friend Lucy whispered to us that she was cancelling her return ticket. She wasn't alone. The only person who didn't seem upset was the drunkard engineer. He sat at the bar every night, drinking and laughing to himself. We thought about cancelling our ticket, but we were a young married couple; we didn't have much money. Our return ticket was our only way home.

The night before we arrived in New York we heard screaming. It was clear, but distant. As if you could hear someone screaming from just over there, inside the nursing home. The moment we landed there was nearly a stampede to get off the ship.

We only spent a few days in New York. It wasn't as long as we'd hoped, but Bill had to get back to work. The city must be so different today, but even then it was an extraordinary place. I'd never seen so many people all at once. And the skyscrapers!

It was almost enough to make us forget about how strange our journey had been. By the time we were getting back on board the ship, we were feeling like maybe somehow we had imagined the whole thing.

That first night, the ballroom was nearly empty. Even some of the musicians had decided not to come back on the return voyage, and those that were left played to drown out the screaming. On the third night, we were woken, the noise was like a loud, dull thud, different to anything we had heard so far. Bill ran out of the cabin. When he finally came back, he was pale as a sheet. "Don't go out there," he said. "A boiler exploded. There were six men in the room. They're all dead."

I went looking for the drunkard who'd haunted the bar on our outward voyage. He had claimed to be an engineer working on the ship, so I wondered if he knew something about the boiler. I couldn't find him. I guessed he must have stayed on shore in New York.

The closer we got to home, the fainter the screaming sounds became, until by the time we were disembarking at Southampton we could hardly hear them at all. They weren't even like screams anymore. Just a faint, desperate whine.

I kept hearing stories about that ship as the years went by. Accidents, people jumping overboard for no reason. People said that it was cursed. One day, Bill looked up from reading the newspaper and told me the ship was gone. It had been coming into port in Hamburg it hit an old mine, and sunk. No one died, thankfully. Still, I was sad. Even though that trip had been the strangest month of my life, it was my honeymoon. That beautiful, state-of-the-art ship. Gone.

Only that wasn't the end of it. When they dragged it up from the sea floor and dismantled it, when they peeled back the double-skinned hull, they found two bodies. Skeletons. Trapped between the outer and the inner hull. And sure enough, two riveters had disappeared during the construction of the ship all those years ago in Genoa. Finally, they had been found.'

Mari breaks off. The group turns towards the stranger who had joined them. He's laughing.

'I'm sorry,' he says. 'I'm sorry to laugh, it's just...' Laughter shakes his ancient frame. His hands wipe away tears of mirth.

'I do know you from somewhere,' says Mari.

'It was a long time ago. I drink less, now. Back then I drank to drown out their screams but now... now you see all I can do is laugh. I remember you from the ballroom. The honeymooners.' The old man leans forward in his seat. 'Do you know how perfectly my designs needed to be executed for that ship to succeed? And all the time I was surrounded by lazy scroungers who refused to pull their weight. Those two were the worst of the lot. It was easy to lure them into the space between the hulls. "Last minute welding," I said. "I'll pay you double." They believed it. Well, it was true in a way. As soon as they were inside I had the hatch welded shut.'

The crowd of old people murmur in discomfort. 'Get away from us,' says one woman. 'You're cursed, like that ship.'

Mari sits very still, an expression of horrified revulsion on her face. The old man shrugs. 'I'm too old for jail,' he says. 'And I already know hell.'

He lifts his black hat in farewell. They watch him walk away across the damp grass. Cleo, the nurse, watches him anxiously. Without warning, the old man lifts his face to the overcast sky, and screams.

'The same sound,' Mari whispers to herself. 'The same voice.'

A Cruise on the Nile

'Well go on, show me.'

Jerry lifted his shirt. Barbara could see the rumpled, crescent-shaped scar running from below his navel up to just below his ribs.

'It makes me feel weird,' Jerry said. 'Like I'm walking around with a secret. Someone else's kidney is in there.'

'It's your kidney now,' said Barbara. 'Come on, I've got a surprise for you.'

Jerry followed Barbara into the study. He was a heavy-set man, approaching sixty, his grey hair starting to thin. But his green eyes were bright and alert – his best feature, Barbara always said. Barbara had aged better. She was slim and fit and moved quickly. She'd cut her honey-brown hair short for the first time two weeks ago and still occasionally lifted a hand to touch it self-consciously. Outside, the afternoon sun was beating against the house. Jerry, who'd lived his whole life in Minnesota, hated the heat. But what Barbara wanted, Barbara got. So two years ago they'd moved back to her hometown of Naples, Florida. Then Jerry got sick.

'Look,' said Barbara, and she handed Jerry a folded piece of paper.

'What's this?'

'You remember I was saying we deserved a holiday? You know, leave the country, be somewhere totally different. To put all this behind us.'

'Yeah?'

'Open it.'

It was a brochure for a cruise along the Nile. On the inside page was a picture of the ship, and written above it: "Travel through time in style and comfort".

'This looks like a pretty old brochure,' said Jerry, peering at the photographs.

'Oh no, they just dress the boat up like it's the 1920s. The crew as well. You know, British colonial style. It seemed like fun.'

Barbara stood with her back to the desk, which was swamped by a disorderly stack of correspondence – doctor's appointments, scans, letters from their insurance company.

'Yeah,' said Jerry, trying to smile. 'Looks like fun. Thank you, sweetheart. You always know just what to do.'

Egypt, Jerry thought to himself. *Perfect. More sun and heat.*

When they arrived, Jerry's first thought was that their tour guide was taking the 1920s theme too far. He bowed and scraped as though a bad word from Jerry or Barbara would get him whipped. He was a small, lean man, his uniform perfectly pressed.

'Welcome,' he said. 'My name is Ammon, please let me help you.'

Jerry handed over the suitcases and they followed Ammon up the ramp.

The ship certainly looked like something out of the 1920s. It was a long barge with two broad decks, and it sat low in the gleaming waters of the Nile. The decks were enclosed by elaborate wrought iron railings, painted white, with soft curtains that could be drawn in the heat of the day. Some of the guests could already be seen sitting at private tables, attended to by the crew. On the far shore, tall palm trees stirred in the breeze. People hurried along the riverfront promenade, coming and going from the bustling modern city of Luxor.

'May I say,' said Ammon as he led them towards their cabin. 'You have chosen the perfect itinerary. Luxor to Aswan is the perfect way to experience the Nile. For myself, I cannot believe my good fortune to have this job. To be paid a salary to experience such wonders every day.'

Barbara smiled, pleased with her choice. The sight of the crew, in their neat uniforms and stylish caps, thrilled her. They passed by the lounge, and Barbara paused to look inside. The room was exquisite; clad in dark wood panels and lined with beautiful old leather couches. The sunlight filtered through wooden shutters so that the whole room was suffused with a soft glow. *Like stepping into a photograph*, she thought.

'Barbara?' said Jerry.

There were shouts from the crew and the boat rocked slightly, and Barbara reached out to steady herself. Ammon smiled back at her. His teeth were very white.

'We have cast off,' he said. 'Today we sail only a very short distance, to Karnak. You will want plenty of time to explore the ancient temple.'

'What about the historic hotel?' Barbara asked, reaching into her pocket for her brochure. 'Karnak's where we stay in the historic hotel, isn't it?'

'Here is your cabin,' said Ammon.

Ammon pushed back the wooden shutters and the sun flooded in. He stood expectantly at the door.

'Oh,' said Jerry, reaching into his pocket. 'I've only got American dollars.'

Ammon took the five-dollar bill, smiling. 'I'll leave you to rest.'

'Didn't he say he was on a salary?' Jerry grumbled, once Ammon had gone. 'What's he doing taking a tip?'

'That's probably just the way they do things here.'

Can you see if they've got air con in this cabin?' said Jerry, wiping his forehead.

Jerry lowered his camera.

'Stand to the left,' he said.

Barbara took a step to the right.

'No, *your* left.'

Barbara stood still, smiling, framed by the hieroglyph-inscribed pillars of the Hypostyle Hall at Karnak.

'Did you get it?' Barbara called. Her voice echoed off the towering pillars.

The shadows of the great columns fell across the pale, ancient pavers. Jerry clicked back through the photographs he had taken earlier that day: Barbara standing under the rough cliffs of the Valley of the Kings and Queens, and on the shore of the Nile, the sunrise spilling across the water. Jerry felt faint. Maybe it was the sun, or maybe just being in these ancient places. The way time seemed to stretch here in Egypt made him dizzy.

Jerry?' said Barbara. 'He's had an operation,' she added, explaining, to Ammon.

'We could go back to the boat,' said Ammon. 'There will be a fantastic Galabeya party on board tonight.'

Jerry shook his head. 'I'm ready for the hotel.'

They made the crossing to the far shore in a felucca; a nimble little boat with a single, blade-like sail. The ochre-colored hills towered above the city. They made Jerry feel uneasy, as if at any moment they might slip and cover the city in ancient rubble. When they landed, Barbara started up the stone steps towards the hotel, but Ammon hurried past and blocked her way.

'Please, Mrs. Shilling, this way.

'But that's the hotel,' said Barbara. 'Its picture is in the brochure.'

Ammon smiled. 'The hotel is closed for renovation.'

'It doesn't look closed,' said Jerry.

'Please, come this way. We have another hotel, just as good.'

Ammon waved a taxi over. Before Barbara could protest, her bag was lifted from her hands and into the taxi. Jerry let himself be guided into the car. He tried to keep in mind what Barbara had said that morning. *That's probably just the way they do things here.*

The new hotel didn't look much like a hotel, more like a large house.

'Where's the hotel sign?' said Jerry.

'Ah, this is a private hotel,' said Ammon.

'I don't see any other tourists, Barbara,' Jerry whispered.

It was true. There were lots of people milling about, but they all seemed to be locals.

'I guess we're getting an authentic experience,' said Barbara.

Their room was even smaller than their cabin. The moment they stepped inside, the door swung shut.

'Ammon?' said Jerry. He hurried to the door, but their guide was gone. The corridor was empty, only their bags were stacked outside their door. 'Is anyone there?'

'Jerry, I have a bad feeling about this,' said Barbara. Jerry leaned against the doorframe, breathing heavily. 'Jerry?'

He slipped into her arms. 'I think I got too much sun,' he said.

Barbara pulled him to the bed. He was so heavy she thought for a moment he wouldn't make it, but then he fell across her knees. He was asleep within moments. Barbara sat in the dark little room, her heart pounding in her chest, trying to ignore the faint sounds of animals scuffling in the rafters above her. She tried to move, but Jerry was too heavy. She was pinned in place. A noise came, just outside their door.

Barbara looked up and noticed for the first time there was no look on the door.

' Hello?' she forced herself to say, trying to keep the fear from her voice. 'Is someone there?'

She could hear someone breathing. But no one answered. *I have to try to stay awake*, she thought.

The sound of knocking on the door woke them both. Barbara gave a little shout of fright as the door opened. Morning sunlight flooded in, and Ammon stood in the doorway, smiling.

'I hope you had a restful night, Mr. and Mrs. Shilling.'

The rest of their trip, Barbara would tell their friends later, was perfect. Barbara and Jerry took things at their own pace, not rushing like they had on that first day.

'Until we arrived in Aswan,' Barbara would explain. 'And then Ammon… well, it was uncomfortable. I feel sorry for him now. He'd been walking around with this secret.'

Arriving in Aswan, as they walked down the ramp Barbara cast a wistful glance back at the boat.

'I feel like everything back home is going to feel so normal by comparison,' she said.

'Looks like someone wants to say goodbye,' said Jerry.

Ammon was hurrying after them. His uniform, usually perfectly pressed, looked ruffled.

'I am sad to be saying goodbye to two such generous guests,' he said.

Jerry sighed and reached into his pocket for a five-dollar bill.

'Please,' said Ammon. 'I am sorry, Mr. Shilling, but can you spare any more? My family and I are in a bad situation.' Ammon glanced nervously back at the boat. 'Please, sir.'

'Go on, Jerry,' said Barbara. 'Ammon's been so good to us.'

Jerry fished in his pockets again. 'That's everything I have on me.'

Ammon quickly hid the money in his coat pocket before walking back onto the boat.

Two weeks after Jerry and Barbara returned home, the phone calls started. They came late at night, from another time zone. Then letters and postcards started arriving from towns all along the Nile, written in halting English.

'There was nothing threatening,' Barbara would say to her friends. 'It was like they wanted just to connect with us. To be friends. But we had no idea how to write back.' At this point, Jerry would always lean across the table. 'Then I looked at my credit card statement. Would you believe – additional charges from that hotel we never stayed in!'

'So I called, didn't I, Jerry, I called the hotel and they hadn't been closed at all. No renovations, nothing. In fact, our room had been sub-rented that night, to complete strangers, and they'd run up a terrible bill on room service. I tried to explain, but no one wanted to listen.'

'So what did you do?'

Jerry shrugged. 'We paid.'

Whenever they told this story to their friends, Jerry ended up thinking about the stranger's kidney in his body. Most days he never thought about it at all. But somehow it gave him the same feeling that he'd had in Egypt. As if he'd been transplanted, put down somewhere different, and somehow had to keep going.

Encounter in the South China Sea

A few years ago, we decided to take our yacht from El Nido, a beautiful beach town of Palawan island, and cross the South China Sea to Da Nang, Vietnam. Once upon a time, this used to be an exclusive route used by moderately sized sailing yachts measuring 20 feet or more. Nowadays, any average Joe with a bit of nautical know-how is bound to want to test their grit on these straits; that's why my husband and I originally thought to try it. We had been sailing for several years, but we were far from experts. In Asia this route is sometimes used for a special kind of race, notably by wealthy Japanese and Chinese living in Singapore who wish to prove their seamanship and bring prestige upon their family name. One of this race's main attractions is the opportunity to skillfully avoid one of the many Chinese military ships which patrol the waters, stationed there in order to safeguard the ports of the occupied Spratly islands. It's a game of high stakes, but success proved something beyond mere seamanship and could elevate one to the heights of a bona fide *pirate*.

We knew that the South China Sea held many pitfalls, but it was supposed to be an experience of a lifetime. We simply could not resist; and besides, we were in the prime of our lives. *Now* was the time for a grand adventure. We took three others with us, a British gentleman who was a veteran sailor with an international reputation, and two Filipino women who would handle all the menial chores aboard our yacht, such as cooking and cleaning. We started out on a very hot day. There was little to no wind, and we were forced to use the reserve engine quite a lot. We were heading east, and the sun set stealthily at our backs. We prepared to bunker down for sleep, in hopes that the morrow would bring more favorable conditions.

"There is no wind," I said to my husband. "I've never seen it so still, on any trip. I really hope our luck changes."

"Don't worry. I've read that it is sometimes this way on the South China Sea. It's enough to make one nervous, but it never lasts for more than a day or two."

I woke in the wee hours that morning and made my way onto the deck. The sky was aglow with constellations, and peace abounded, but there was still not a scrap of wind. Despite what my husband said, I was beginning to grow nervous.

That day, we discovered that we'd miscalculated our fuel levels. If no wind soon came, we'd need to turn around, or else drift aimlessly, which was not a reassuring alternative. By late afternoon of the same day, we began to experience engine problems. Our little inboard prop was overheating because we had been running it so hard. The British veteran began cursing us for being novices, and I thought at one point he was going to knock my husband clear off the deck. He had begun drinking copious amounts of rum, which made him a real handful rather than an asset.

Luckily around this time we spotted a boat in the distance. It looked to be making straight for us, thank the Lord. As it got closer, we realized it was a Chinese vessel, some sort of military speedboat which zipped across the top of the water at a considerable clip. They began making hand signs to us, but my husband and I could not discern what it was they wanted. The Brit staggered over, and though now dimwitted from booze, told us that they were using international signals which basically spelled *turn around*.

But we could not comply, though we would have gladly done so. See, our engine was overheated and there was still no wind to speak of. The Brit tried to convey this to the

Chinese via a series of complicated gestures, and eventually the boat turned around and disappeared. We thought they had understood, and we all breathed a sigh of relief.

That night, while everyone aboard was fast asleep, there was an incredible crash, a ringing din that woke everyone with a start. Panicking, we rushed onto the deck. It was the Chinese vessel again, and it had rammed our yacht and thoroughly breached the hull. As the Chinese boat disappeared into the night, we realized that we were rapidly taking water. We tried to use the emergency repair kit to close the gap in the hull, but the kit was reserved for small punctures and tears. It helped very little and the yacht was in peril. All the electrical equipment became saturated, and we had no way to contact help. We could think of nothing to do but don life vests and sit on the deck. We prayed, but we all knew our time was short. The two Filipino ladies huddled in a corner and quietly wept, while my husband and I only stared over the darkening water in disbelief. The Brit was resigned to his bottle, a worthy companion for such a grim fate.

When true night fell, we saw shark fins circling the boat, as if they possessed primal intuition about the fate of our craft. Luckily, with the coming of the sun, another vessel appeared on the horizon, which did not seem to be the dreaded Chinese military ship.

As it drew alongside us, the two Filipino women started a merry, bird-like chorus, for it was a Filipino craft, namely a fishing vessel, piloted by a group of strapping young men. They swiftly took us aboard, and not too soon, for our yacht was nearly underwater. The two Filipino women embraced our saviors, and we issued our thanks, though somewhat gruffly and with an air of conceit. We thought they would take us back towards El Nido, but instead the fishermen took us to a small, unknown island, which they claimed was better "for the likes of us". The Filipino women stayed on the fishing vessel, while my husband and I, along with the Brit, got off on the little island that appeared a literal paradise.

We were quite amazed, as there were other people on this island, a group of Japanese men who all looked ragged and exhausted, like castaways. They explained to us, while we all gathered around a fire fed by dung, that they had had a similar experience. Their vessel was also rammed by a Chinese ship of military origin, and they had managed to make it here on a lifeboat. They told us that while the island was beautiful and verdant, it was not inhabited, and there seemed to be little in the way of food or fresh water. They had quickly grown malnourished due to this fact.

Maintaining a diet only of indigenous nuts and dirty water drawn from a nearby stream, my husband and I soon became weak. Our health deteriorated by the hour; we slept fitfully through the day, and at night were both in the throes of fever dreams. I barely recall a single thing during that time, though I have this fleeting image of a wizened old Japanese man feeding us a strange concoction whose consistency was not unlike oatmeal.

One morning, we were woken by someone prodding us with their boots. Men in fancy, well-pressed uniforms stood over us. They informed us that they were Filipino customs officers, and that they had a boat which would take us back to the mainland. We found two of the Japanese "castaways" already on board, but we did not see our British veteran. Perhaps he had drunk himself to death; to this day I know nothing of his whereabouts.

An hour into the voyage back to Palawan island, one of the customs officers pulled me aside.

"Miss, do you know how long you and your husband were on that island?"

"Why, I can't say for sure, I feel like it was a lifetime…but that can't be. We were quite ill. I think we became delirious. It's hard to say."

"I wanted to ask you about the bones. We found countless skeletons, all human. It was like a great ritual had taken place; the kind of sacrifice to the gods my people made in bygone times."

I said that I couldn't tell him a thing. I knew of no bones nor sacrifices, but that I had prayed heartily to God and devil alike. I only remember that we were hungry all the time.

Chapter IV

Uplifting Short Novels of Faith

A Strange Dream

Since I got off the pills, I sleep deeper. Of course, I had been taking the tablets for years, but it was no longer possible, I had to get off them. Nothing else happened, but my life became better, especially physically. My sleep was no longer like a coma and was again filled with dreams, but more real, more fantastic, sometimes strange, but I usually couldn't remember them.

Then the other day, I had another dream. In this dream, I found myself in a strange room. There were no special features there, except a wall littered with small old-fashioned index card boxes, similar to those found in libraries in the past. But these card boxes, of which there seemed to be an endless number, had extraordinary titles.

When I approached the card index boxes, the first one that caught my eye had the words, 'Girl I once liked' written on it. I pulled out the drawer and started leafing through the records. At that moment, I pushed the drawer back again. I was shocked because I immediately recognized the names written there. And then, without having been told, I suddenly knew exactly where I was.

This lifeless room with all its small index cards was an unembellished cataloging system of my life. All the deeds and thoughts of my life were recorded here in such detail that my memory could not come close to keeping up with them.

A feeling of amazement and curiosity, mixed with horror, pervaded me as I began to randomly open different boxes and examine their contents. Some of them brought me joy and pleasant memories. Others I felt ashamed of, for they brought a feeling of remorse, so intense that I looked over my shoulder to see if I was being observed.

There was a file called 'Friends' next to a file called 'Friends I betrayed'. There were all kinds of different files. Some were absolutely ordinary, such as, 'Books I read', Jokes I laughed at'. Some were rather strange like, 'School hours I slept in', 'Favorite objects of my mother I broke', 'Work I shirked'. Some were really funny in terms of their accuracy, 'Nasty things I threw at my brother's head', others I couldn't laugh at all. 'Things I did in anger', 'Quarrels I started'.

I was always surprised by the contents of the index card boxes. Often there were many more index cards than I expected, then again, sometimes less than I had hoped to find. Nevertheless, I was amazed by the amount of information about the life I've lived. Could it be possible that in all the years I had created each of these thousands, even millions of cards myself? So far, every card confirmed that assumption. They were all written in my handwriting — they all bore my signature.

When I pulled out the index card, 'Songs I have heard', I saw no end to it. The cards were tightly packed, and seemed endless. Ashamed, I closed the box again, not because of the quality of the music, but rather because of the vast amount of time I had wasted, as it was so clear by now.

When I came to a file entitled 'Lustful thoughts', I felt a shiver running through my limbs. I pulled the box out an inch or two, not wanting its full length revealed to me. I pulled out a card. I shivered when I noticed its detailed contents.

I felt sick at the thought that such a moment had been recorded. I felt anger and panic rising within me. A single thought dominated in my head, *Never let anyone see these cards! No one must ever see this room! I absolutely must destroy all this.*

In an almost insane rage, I tore the box out of the wall. Its size was no longer important. I had to empty it and burn the cards. I took the box in one swing and smashed it on the floor, but then, like in a nightmare nothing, no cards came loose. Desperately I tried to rip out a single card with both hands, but my endeavor was futile, for it was anchored and unbreakable. Weary and totally helpless, I shoved it back into the box.

With my arms down by my sides and my head resting against the wall, I stood there and sighed out loud with pity. All of this could not be true. And then I saw it. The title was, 'People to whom I have brought the Gospel'.

This box looked better than the others, newer, almost unused. I wanted to pull it out, but there wasn't much to pull out of it. I could count the cards with the finger of one hand. My eyes filled with tears. Somehow I started to cry, with a sob so deep that it hurt my stomach and shook me completely. I cried out in pain from the overwhelming shame I felt. The index card boxes blurred before my tear-filled eyes.

No one — no one must ever know about this room. I must lock it up and hide the key where no one can find it. But then for a split second, it occurred to me. What if this all was just a dream, what if I could still make amends? What if I could continue to bring the Gospel out? The outcome would be different, for sure, probably the indexes would be arranged differently, most likely the whole room would be different. And with the grasp of this thought, I didn't want this alternative outcome to be a dream. I wanted to become this reality.

Puppies for Sale

A shop owner had nailed a sign over his door that read 'Puppies for sale'. The sign attracted children. Soon a little boy appeared and asked, "How much do they sell the babies for?"

The owner said, "Between 30 and 50 dollars."

The little boy reached into his pocket and pulled out some change. "I have two and a quarter, can I have a look at them?"

The owner grinned and whistled. Out of the kennel came a dog named Lady, she ran down the aisle of his shop, followed by five puppies. One of them was walking alone, visibly far behind the others. Immediately the boy saw the limping little one and asked, "What's wrong with this little dog?"

The man explained that when the little one was born, the vet said it had broken a joint and would limp for the rest of its life.

The little boy yelled out excitingly, "Let me have him. I want to buy that little dog!"

The man replied, "No, you don't want to buy the little dog. If you really want the puppy, I'll give it to you."

The little boy was confused. He looked straight into the man's eyes and said, "I don't want the puppy as a gift. It's worth as much as the other dogs, and I want to pay full price. I'll give you what I've got now, and pay you 10 dollars every month until I pay off my debt."

The man shook his head. "You really don't have to pay for this dog, son. It'll never be able to run, bounce or play like the other little dogs."

The boy reached down and rolled up the leg of his pants, and showed his badly bent, crippled left leg, splinted with a thick metal bar.

He looked up at the man and said, "Listen, I can't run very well either, and the little dog needs someone who'll understand it."

The man bit his lower lip. Tears came to his eyes, he smiled and said, "My son, I hope and pray that each one of these little puppies will have an owner like you."

Great Expectations

In 1988, my then-wife, Suzy, and I were on vacation in Hawaii when she landed a publication deal for her first novel: Inside the Bathroom. It was with a reputable publisher that was still in business at that time.

Looking back, I can honestly say that my good memory saved her manuscript. But I don't want to get ahead of myself, so let me tell you what happened to us from the beginning.

It all started with a kind of secret vacation, because our extended family has always been—and still is—suspicious about our income. After all, I'm officially in real estate, and Suzy is a writer, both of us with unknown success. Actually, we're a humble couple who occasionally seeks financial help from various family members. So, no one needed to know that we were flying towards Hawaii. Truthfully, to this day, Hawaii is known to us as the island of impending disaster.

Anyway, on this rather misty morning, the two of us sat completely alone on a secluded beach, just us and our folding chairs.

I was comfortably reading a book. Actually, it was Suzy's manuscript, because I like to help her, not because I give a shit about her smelly stories. Still, this story wasn't bad, and I was the first man to read it. And yes, I told how proud I was of her for being an accomplished writer. I tried to focus on my reading when I was suddenly interrupted by her voice:

"Honey, there isn't much water today."

"Let me finish this," I said.

"Honey... please, take a look."

I stared at the wide beach... no water. Not even people.

"It's got to be ebb," I said.

"But it looks so strange. Do they really have tides like that here?"

I stood up, trying to remember the page. No water? So what?

"Suzy, this is surely just ebb. You need to walk about 200 yards, then you'll find water."

"Weird..."

"No, look behind us, there are some people walking on the beach, and all are in a jolly mood."

"Looks like they're waving their arms."

"I don't care. Let me finish this page, okay?"

I almost doze off when suddenly, some rough hand begun shaking my shoulder.

"Suzy, what's going on?"

"Honey, what's all that water doing there? Look!"

"Let me just doze another minute," I said.

"Why?"

Then I saw it myself, indeed there was a lot of water coming rolling towards us, waves with a lot of white foam on top. I jumped to my feet and abruptly pull Suzy up with both hands.

"Run!" I yell. "There's a tsunami coming!"

"You mean we've got a flood coming?"

I started running, drawing her behind me. "Run faster," I scream.

"Not so fast, Harry! I'm stumbling!"

Just in time, a minute or so later, we made it to the beach hotel. We ran straight up to the fourth floor to our balcony. We could already hear the noise and screams.

The sight from the balcony was indescribable. There was a fast-flowing stream of mud and water sweeping inland, and our hotel was surrounded by all kinds of debris. There was devastation everywhere.

There was nothing we could do. Suzy seemed to be in shock, and she laid down on the bed.

Something popped into my mind, and I shook my head.

"Susy, wake up."

"Oh my God, Al. What can we do?"

"Now, I will never know," I said.

"What's that?"

I kneeled in front of the bed. "How the novel ended. I left it on the beach."

I looked at her face and could clearly recognize tears running down her cheeks.

"Harry," she cried. "That was my only manuscript!"

"Don't worry, sweetie," I said. "It was so good that I memorized every line, seriously."

Living in Nature

My husband and I decided years ago to live in the country. A lot of things led to that decision back then, but that was a long time ago now, and on this quiet morning, I started the day by taking a short walk into the nearby forest.

Of course, I always need a few minutes to understand and really experience this small change from our simple dwelling to the gentle nature.

The footpath started outside our property, where the path narrowed down, surrounded by dense bushes and tall trees. If I hadn't known better, I might have thought I was lost in the wilderness.

And there it stood, a tall spruce at the edge of the clearing. In this neighborhood, there were others like it, as well as other types of trees of all sizes. Together they painted a beautiful picture, especially shortly after sunrise, when the dew still glittered freshly on the needles and leaves. The blackbirds that had sung to themselves a little earlier were accompanied by other chamber singers, and the first mosquitoes began circling around the tips of the branches.

At the foot of the spruce, the ants had created a mighty hill in the last few weeks. A few steps further into the clearing, in an old dead tree trunk surrounded by delicate purple Bellflowers, the small swarm of hornets had by now developed into a real state and were using the narrow forest path that ran by the spruce as their main flight route.

Only yesterday a pair of Pine Warblers had accepted the wide-spreading branches of the spruce as a welcome invitation to build a well-protected nest high up in its branches.

If nothing extraordinary happened, this would considerably increase in size in the coming years due to its construction.

Usually, one could feel pure life here on all floors — under, between and above the forest trees. This was why hikers and even hunters paused reverently again and again. They would close their eyes, breath in deeply and relax, as they tried to capture this precious moment deep into their hearts for eternity. They could then feed on this magical experience again with closed eyes in the hectic everyday life.

One rainy evening a dragonfly appeared between the dripping branches. On its flight home to the nearby pond, it had been surprised by the rain and had sought shelter under the broad branches for a while.

It started bragging about one of its last trips to the nearby outskirts of the city, leaving those in the audience who knew nothing about it in open amazement. Yes, the dragonfly had also seen a fir tree there. However, this one had been much more colorful, standing alone, as crowds of dancing and celebrating people had surrounded it. Yes, white and blue ribbons with flags and garlands had hung down from its proud branches, it was simply indescribable. It was indeed stately and imposing to look at. The tree was so radiantly beautiful that another dragonfly almost flew into a light pole. Moreover, people would always put up new trees of this kind, which they had previously carefully selected in the forest.

To be such a magnificent tree once in a lifetime would finally be something meaningful, thought the spruce, given all that the dragonfly had said. No longer to be one of many trees living day after day half-hidden here at the edge of the forest, having to live such a bounded existence. Colorful ribbons instead of bird droppings, garlands instead of swarms of mosquitoes and dancing children instead of dead caterpillars and beetles and ants. Yes, this must be the true fulfillment for every tree, absolutely!

Deep inside, the tree had been asking itself for a long time, what the meaning of its existence could be and also if it were possible to step out of the shadow of the other trees and realize itself in a different way.

Time can pass more slowly in the country, it seems. I remember last autumn, which came a few days later, bringing a firework of reds and yellows to the clearing, as well as the countless leaves and fruits.

However, when winter came with its mass of snow taking a few branches from the tree, the desire of last summer became so overwhelming that I almost overlooked the first anemones in early March. These greeted the onsets of spring, between the now snow-free foliage and a thick layer of needles.

But even the warming rays of the sun, the bees busily flying around in the pastures as well as the butterflies dancing above the sky could no longer fill the emptiness that was like a constant and desolate companion.

One morning a loud roar could be heard from afar, followed by its smell. A small group of cheerful men with ropes and chains followed the exhaust clouds of a tractor. I only recognized the strange-looking object in the back of the tractor at the last moment. It was a chainsaw.

What could they be doing with that machine out here at such an early hour?

Still absorbed in these considerations, I noticed that the group of workers had come to a halt right in front of the large spruce tree. One of the men pointed directly at it and at its mighty trunk, whereupon all the others nodded in agreement.

We watched the massacre from a distance, at least what we could see of it.

After they had removed the spruce, we saw the heron's nest hanging destroyed in the neighboring tree, and the anthill totally trampled. Not only did the pair of herons have to build a new nest on such short notice but the smaller trees were left without shelter. They were now fully exposed to the wind and rain and would grow more slowly and bent by the elements.

My husband told me that I was too sensitive. He also taught me that nature is just constant adaptation, it is creative, explosive in its power and full of life energy, and regenerates itself. He also told me that this principle should apply to people and that we should always make the best of things. The main thing is that we are happy.

In any case, I never saw the workers again, and where the old stump stood, hundreds of small fresh shrubs, mushrooms and young flower stems blossomed — the old wood had come to life once more.

My husband died last month, and since we lived alone, I buried him in a secret place in the forest, not far from the old spruce, where a small gentle mound of earth, which I shoveled by myself, still stood and was now blooming in March like a small natural paradise. There was no other place that could boast small flowers and blades of grass as juicy as on the unrecognizable heap of earth.

Since I know how beautiful the blooming is in this place, I sit here more often and enjoy nature. Sometimes, between the branches and leaves, a light appears. From a certain distance, it resembles a translucent figure wearing a type of white cape. I sometimes think I even recognize the face of a man who knows me and smiles.

Chapter V

After Decades in the Bedroom - Humorous Anecdotes

25 Years

Ellen and her husband Bob went for counseling after 25 years of marriage. When asked what the problem was, Ellen went into a passionate, painful tirade listing every problem they had ever had in the 25 years they had been married. She went on and on and on: neglect, lack of intimacy, emptiness, loneliness, feeling unloved and unlovable, an entire laundry list of unmet needs she had endured over the course of their marriage. Finally after allowing this to go for a sufficient length of time, the therapist got up, walked around the desk and after asking Ellen to stand, embraced her, unbuttoned her blouse, and quietly sat down while basking in the glow of being highly aroused. The therapist turned to bob and said "This is what your wife needs at least three times a week. Can you do this??"

Bob thought for a moment and replied, "Well I can drop off here on Mondays Wednesdays, but Fridays I play golf."

She Gave him a Short Story Instead

It has almost become a tradition for Marta and Harry to meet up with other pensioners at the country club for a charity game evening. Both have an urge to meet like-minded retirees but of course Harry also wants to win, just for his self-affirmation that he still has what it takes.

At seven o'clock sharp, the cab picks them up. Across the vast golf fields, Harry can already make out the clubhouse in the distance. "You know darling" he says slightly amused, "I have a feeling I am going to get cheated tonight."

Marta stares into his face. "Then you shouldn't even start to gamble."

"Maybe it won't be about the gambling," he replied, smirking.

The cab stops and a valet parker opens the door. But this is not the usual valet parker, Harry is totally perplexed by this voluptuous woman in red tight sports pants and bright toxic-blond hair.

As Marta saunters toward the entrance, the tall blonde pulls Harry aside and whispers. "Sweety, If you play your cards right, we can have a little more fun in the men's room afterwards."

"Really...," Harry stammers.

She whispers in his ear. "Only 50 for short time honey."

Harry nods, keeping his eyes focused straight ahead. "Okay! But don't tell my wife."

She winks at him with a smile.

From a distance, Marta waves at him. "Hurry up darling, they've already started."

Almost a bit hidden in an annex of the otherwise quite plush club are two large conference tables with red cloth sheets, surrounded by curious and ambitious retirees, ready to join in on the Carnival Game. Actually, it's a so-called bean bag leap carnival game. In this game the players toss bean bags that have a frog design to land on lily pads with different values. For Marta it's a stupid game but for Harry it's more an opportunity of economic happiness .

Marta shakes her head in disgust. "Why are you so serious with that game Harry?"

"It's just today I need to win!"

"Why? It's just a game."

He almost whispers. "I really need the money."

Marta distance herself from the table, this is all too much for her, instead, she prefers to eat apple pie standing up and talking to other seniors about their illnesses.

It completely escapes Marta's attention that Harry has a winning streak, and as a result has already received companionship. The tall blonde was back and sits down close to Harry.

Harry has a real run, the only thing that stops him from winning is his almost constant urge to go to the bathroom.

The blonde whispers in his ear while slightly touching his knee. "Let' go, Honey, I suck you in the bathroom."

"You know what, I actually have to go to the bathroom, but for my own reasons."

"Take your time Harry"

As soon as Harry gets up, the blonde sneaks up behind him, unobtrusively darting into the men's room.

Harry is totally shocked when he turns around and the tall blonde is staying in front of him, pressing her finger slightly on his libs. "Shh," she whispers and is already getting ready to unzip his pants.

"Oh my God," Harry grunts.

Then she turns around and sits down on the toilet. "You can just stay there; I do the rest".

Harry closes his eyes, now he's expecting it, her lips on his....but then it pops into his mind that what's happening now may be the last time in his life.

But for long seconds nothing happens, and Harry keeps his eyes closed....still nothing. Then he hears her voice, "Give me hundred dollar now."

"You said it's 50."

"100! C'mon Harry."

"It's in my pocket."

The blonde pulls the note out of his pants and whispers. "You know Harry…"

"What?"

"I was going to Church this morning…."

"Ah… excuse me?"

"The pastor told me I had to atone for my sins."

"What sins?"

"See Harry, I am the mother of 5 children…. And I used to work in an establishment down at the port."

"Honey I thought you are giving me …you know…."

But she interrupts. "Harry, my ex was an alcoholic, and now he passed away. And my mother, you know, she is 87 years old, so she must be just a few years older than you."

"Honey why are you telling me all this?"

"Harry are you listening to me?"

"I try…"

"Then keep your eyes closed and listen."

"I am listening."

"…By the way, have you seen my handbag?"

Suddenly a knock on the door. Voices. "Excuse me, what's going on in there?"

Harry is shocked and confused, carefully he opens the door. Then he feels his jaw dropping, right outside the toilet there's a whole group of people staying in a semicircle, they all stare at him in disbelief, and Marta stares at him like he's insane.

Suddenly the Blonde rushes out and screams: "I sinned, I sinned!"

Marta sinks down onto the floor and starts crying while the others are whispering and shaking their head in disgust.

Carefully Harry closes his fly as he hears the voice of the club director. "Harry.. I can't even begin to express how disappointed I am.."

But then the Blonde interrupts and shouts, "It's all my fault! I cheated on Harry! I took his money, promised him *felaciao* and gave him a short story instead!"

Pension Insurance

A man has turned 65 and goes to the pension insurance scheme to submit his application. He takes a number in the waiting room and waits to be called.

Shortly before his waiting number is called, he realizes that he has forgotten his ID. It's too late to get him, so he waits his turn.

His number is called and he enters the office.

"Hello, sorry, I forgot my ID!"

The lady replies, "It doesn't matter. Pull up your t-shirt!"

The man is surprised, but does as requested. When the woman sees the graying hair on her chest, she says: "That's enough. You're at least 65! You'll get a pensioner's card."

After the formalities are done, the man goes home and tells his wife. She only looks at him briefly and says: "If you had let down your pants, you would have gotten a disability card..."

The Local Pub

Every year a few friends get together to have a great evening in the local pub.

When they turned 40, they met and puzzled over what to do that night. They didn't agree at first, but then someone said:

"Let's go to the local pub, the waitress is hot and always wears a low-cut blouse!" Said and done.
Ten years later, when they turned 50, they met again and again puzzled over what to do that night. They disagreed again at first, but then one said:

"Let's go to the local pub, you eat very well there and the wine list has a few fine drops to offer!" Said and done.

Ten years later, when they turned 60, they met again and again puzzled over what to do that night. Again they disagreed at first, but then one said:

"Let's go to the local pub it's quiet there and nobody smokes!" Said and done.
Ten years later, when they turned 70, they met again and again puzzled over what to do that night. As every year, they didn't agree at first, but then someone said:

"Let's go to the local pub, everything is wheelchair accessible and there is a lift!" Said and done...

They recently turned 80, met again and puzzled over what to do that night. They didn't agree at first, but then one said: "Let's go to the local pub"

Then another said: "Good idea, we've never been there!"

In the Drugstore

Jane and Arlene are outside their nursing home, having a drink and a smoke, when it starts to rain. Jane pulls out a condom, cuts off the end, puts it over her cigarette, and continues smoking.

Arlene: "What in the hell is that?"

Jane: "A condom. This way my cigarette doesn't get wet?"

Arlene: "Where did you get it?"

Jane: "You can get them at any drugstore."

The next day, Arlene hobbles herself into the local drugstore and announces to the pharmacist that she wants a box of condoms. The pharmacist, obviously embarrassed, looks at her kind of strangely, she is after all over 80 years of age, but very delicately asks what brand of condoms she prefers. "Doesn't matter Sonny, as long as it fits on a Camel". The pharmacist fainted.

The Thai Mother In-Law

The Thai mother in-law walks into her daughter's new house in the village and finds her *Farang* son-in-law furious and packing his suitcase.

"What happen? She asked.

"What happened? – I'll tell you what happened! I sent an e-mail to my wife Kai saying that I was coming home from England today. I got here and guess what I found? My wife Kai, yes your daughter, in our bed with a Thai gentlemen! This is the end of our marriage and I am leaving Thailand forever!"

"Relax, relax", says mother in-law. Mistake sure! Something is not right about the story. Kai never would do something so stupid! Wait....I check to see what really happen." Moments later she comes back with a big smile. "See I told you there must be a simple explanation.... Kai never receive your e-mail."

Her Name was Rosie

Ronald celebrated his 55th birthday today alone with his dog socks and a sixpack of Pepsi. Because it has been six years that he had been dry. And not Coke, because the cans had this irritating color red.

For Ronald, the color red was the color of love, of memories, and red invigorated her senses. He also had a neighbor named Rosie. And Rosie was special, then as now.

At Ronald's and in fact at all the neighbors, Rosie was even known to bake special rose cakes,

Ronald imagined that his special neighbor, that on the street where all the trailer houses look pretty much the same, that Rosie had brought a special flair to the neighborhood, however, in private, Ronald had a slightly different opinion of Rosie, which is why that he had known her intimate side a long time ago. In fact, he'd had the experience that Rose even stank of rose oil, everything about her smelled of grease and her breath smelled of a kind of vanilla, but that was all the past now, at least back then she wasn't quite as obese as she is now. Still, she was pretty damn attractive in her own way. If there was one person he had the best sex with ever, it was Rosie!

But back then he didn't care, he was a bit younger back then, and back then he didn't care about almost anything about women, as long as they were fucking and as long as she was wet. Funny these thoughts after all this time, he thought. And now Ronald remembered: They only made the love in his house, he was never invited to hers! Actually, her house was very different, like there was a secret inside. Interestingly, Rosie had recently the house freshly painted.

But despite all the memories and everything, Ronald was sure that there was something was wrong in her house, something terrible wrong! And of course there something was something wrong with Rosie.

But Ronald didn't want to worry too much about Rosie, he had enough problems on his own. Actually, he had hit the bottom with 55, he knew that for a fact, because today was his birthday. He had no job to speak of, no family and no one to turn to, and his business as a dog breeder still had not recovered since the pandemic, and no prospect of recovery, except he occasionally thought of Rosie, the good old times, perhaps she could help?

It was getting dark by the time Ronald sat in the rocking chair on the porch with only a Pepsi in hand, which was okay as he felt the compulsion to look at Rosie's house. As always, in the darkness mysterious lights flickered through the windows.

The street seemed to be unusual busy, cars came, small trucks and vans were passing by all the time. Ronald shook his head in confusion when suddenly a man stepped onto the porch and silently threw a card at his feet. Before Ronald could say anything, the man was already gone.

Now totally confused, Ronald picked up the card and discovered it was a birthday card. *Happy 55* it said, and there was a picture on the back – roses! Ronald couldn't believe it, he had just thought of her, and now, totally unexpected she send him a birthday card, yes, good old Rosie was the only one who wished him a happy birthday!

The next morning, as soon as Ronald got out of bed, he jumped into his truck and sped full throttle into town. He stormed into the flower shop and ordered the largest bouquet of flowers he'd ever held in his hand. All roses! Yes, today he had the chance and opportunity to win back his old flame

Rosie, this was the chance to impress her, after all she made the first move by sending him a birthday card.

Tires squealing, Ronald pulled up in front of Rosie's house, pounding at the door with his fist: "Open up, it' Ron!"

Unexpectedly, the door opened just a crack, a Mexican woman looked at him curiously. "You want to see Senora Rosa?"

"Hey what's going on here, Rosie are you there?"

"Let him in", a familiar voice said.

Ronald stormed into the room. His eyes winded, he couldn't make sense of what he saw.

Finally Rosie appeared, she smiled like an angel. "Hi Ron, nice to see you, and I see you brought as more merchandise."

"What?"

"The roses. As you can see what got plenty here."

Ronald narrowed his eyes, then realized the reality. The whole house was packed with roses, rose petals, stems, bottles, containers, boxes and even some food processors.

"Come here," Rosie said, slightly amused. "As you can see, I have a business, we make rose oil here, for perfume, for creams and essences to smell." Rosie held out her palm to him. "Here smell it, our latest creation:"

In an instant Ronald turned around, ran out and threw up right outside the entrance.

A Special Dance

I am getting on in years and not the best looking guy
anymore. Some would even say I'm a little frayed around the
edges. But I have a nice car, a little money, and I spend most
of my time casually traveling from place to place and
enjoying live. I met a nice looking girl in the park the other
evening. There was an instant spark between us. All of a
sudden, she did this cute little dance, then immediately
dropped to her knees and lie on the grass at my feet. As we
lay there making love I thought…"Wow, these taser guns a
really worth the money."

Chapter VI

Elderly Couples Jokes and Essays

An older man carefully steps onto the ice surface, walks a bit into the middle, takes out a hatchet, chops a hole in the ice, sits down and holds his fishing rod in the hole. Then a deep voice sounds from above; "There's nothing to fish for here."

The man looks around and when he sees nothing, he continues fishing. Again the voice sounds; "There is nothing to fish here."

He looks around again, nothing. Exasperated, he calls out, "Who is speaking there? God?"

To which the voice responds, "The spokesman for the ice rink."

Granny and his granddaughter are having coffee and cake. He says, "In hindsight, I have to admit that I have experienced and suffered so much more than my fellow human beings can even imagine, and it wasn't that easy to get up from the bottom in those difficult times that my generation was exposed to .

The granddaughter looks at him curiously. "Those must have been exciting times, why don't you write it all down in a book?"

"Good idea," says Granny. "However, there were some things that were very difficult and also embarrassing."

"Now I have an important question, Grandpa."

"Tell me your question."

"What were those embarrassing things grandpa?" Granny thinks for a moment. "And that's all I have to say about it, next question please."

A pensioner comes to the doctor and says: "Hey doc, my wife is only 35, I'm already 75 and yet she got pregnant! How can that be?"

Doctor: "Imagine you are walking in the woods, you see a rabbit, you take your stick and you pretend to shoot the rabbit and it falls over. What do you think?"

"Someone else shot!"

"I agree."

17-year-old Anne says to her friend: "It was true when my grandpa told me not to go to the nightclub. Things would happen there that are nothing to my eyes." The girlfriend asked curiously: "What did you see so great?" "My grandpa!"....

Grandma Helga is sitting in the bus. Across from her sits a teenager who is constantly chewing gum. Grandma Helga watches him for a long time with strained eyes and then says: Please excuse me, but if you want to tell me something, you have to speak louder, because I'm hard of hearing.

An elderly couple is dining in an elegant Michelin-star restaurant. The waiter approaches the table and turns to the lady: "Has it escaped your attention that your husband has just slipped under the table?

No, no, not possible. My husband has just come in the door.

Man at the doctor's: Mr. Doctor, how can I live to be 100?

His doctor replies: Do you smoke?

The health-conscious patient: No.

Do you eat excessively?

No.

Do you go to bed late?

No.

Do they have affairs?

No.

The doctor replies, slightly annoyed: "Then tell me, why do you want to get so old anyway?

An elderly lady is walking through the city park after grocery shopping, as she does every afternoon, when a man suddenly jumps out of the bushes. He opens his brown long coat in front of her and wants to scare the poor lady. The lady takes a short look at the man, then says: Holy crab, I forgot to buy eggs.

When Marri was young, she had been invited to many weddings from all her wider family and friends. But every time all her uncles, aunts, grandparents and grandparents-to-be, pricked her with their fingers in the side and legs. They said always the same thing. Your are next, …you are next… and…. You got to be next.

It only stopped when Marri did the same thing to them at funerals.

A wife woke up her husband in the middle of the night and told him, "Dear, there seems to be a burglar in the house. Wake up!" But her husband refused to go out and investigate. "Why are you scared?" she said. "I thought you were brave when you married me!"

"Well yes, that's what my buddies said, too."

A woman was complaining to the neighbor that her husband always came home late, no matter how she tried to stop him. "Take my advice," said the neighbor, "..and do what I did. Once my husband came home at three o'clock in the morning, and from my bed I called out: 'Is that you Jim?' And that cured him."

"That cured him?" asked the woman, incredulous. "But how?"

The neighbor said, "You see, his name is Bill."

"Sugar why don't you sit down by the table and well start supper," said Dorothy to her husband 50 of years.

"Sure thing," said her husband, settling himself down. "Now darling, would you like the soup first or the salad?" asked Dorothy.

"Umm I guess I'll take the soup." He responded.

After a whole meal of one endearing term after another their guest Bob couldn't contain his curiosity any longer. Bob snuck into the kitchen and asked, "Dorothy do you always talk to your husband like that?"

"Bob, I'll be honest with you." Dorothy replied. "It's been five years now, I just can't remember his name, and I am just too embarrassed to ask him!"

And old man went to the doctor complaining of a terrible pain in his leg.

"I am afraid it's just old age," replied the doctor.

"There can't be," fumed the old man. "You don't know what you are doing."

"How can you possible know I am wrong?" countered the doctor.

"Well it's quite obvious," the old man replied. "My other leg is fine, and it's the exact same age!"

On the way between the church and the cemetery, the funeral procession passes a lake where an angler is sitting. He sees the procession, stands up, takes off his hat and bows to the funeral procession. After the funeral, the priest passes the lake again on his way back, goes to the fisherman and tells him that he thought it was a very decent gesture on his part. The fisherman says: "You know, Father, it's the least you can do when you've been married for thirty years".

70-year-old Susi is standing next to her old Cadillac convertible with her old school friend Karen, desperately trying to open the door with a wire.
"Damn it, I told you not to close the door because I left the key in it," Susi scolds.
"Don't get upset," Karen says in a huff. "You better hurry up, it looks like it's about to start raining."
My God, you're right," Susi says as she looks up at the sky.
"Then I'd better put the top up before the leather seats get wet."

The elderly lady Sabrina wants to fly on vacation and has sat down in the business class despite her ticket for the economy class. A flight attendance notices the cheeky attempt and asks her to move to economy class. The elderly lady persistently remains seated. A second flight attendance tries, but the elderly lady still remains seated. The flight attendants don't know what to do and call the pilot. He goes to the elderly lady and talks to her briefly. To the astonishment of the crew, the elderly lady takes her things and sits down in economy class. A flight attendants asks the pilot. "How did you do that?"

The pilot replies: "I told her that business class doesn't fly to Florida."

Toni's father is walking through the apartment in the evening when he hears Toni praying in his room: "Dear God, please protect my mom, my dad, my grandma and my grandpa." The next evening, the father walks past Toni's door again when he hears: "Dear God, please protect my mum, my dad and my grandma." The father notices that Toni hasn't listed grandpa. When the father comes home from work the next day, he learns that the grandfather fell down the stairs and died.

In the evening the father walks past Toni's room again, he hears Toni say: "Dear God, please protect my mum and dad." The father notices that this time Toni didn't list Grandma. The next day the father comes home and the grandma has died of a heart attack.

Surprised, the father waited in front of Toni's door that evening to hear what Toni was praying: "Dear God, please protect my mom." For fear of dying, the father watches out all day long. When he finally gets home, he asks if there's anything new.

His wife says: "Yes, haven't you heard? The postman died!"

George wakes up after a night of drinking with a terrible hangover. On his bedside table he finds a headache tablet and a glass of water. Next to it is a small note that says: "Darling, breakfast is in the kitchen, I just went shopping. I love you. George takes a tablet and drags himself into the kitchen. There he finds a lovingly laid breakfast table, the daily newspaper is ready for him, and his son is sitting there calmly eating.

George asks him: "Tell me, son, what did actually happened yesterday?

"Oh, daddy, you came home in the middle of the night and were totally drunk. You destroyed the wardrobe, threw up in the hallway and hit your head on the door frame."

"But why is everything so tidy here and breakfast prepared?" asks George, confused.

"That's nothing," the son answers. Mom took you into the bedroom and heaved you onto the bed. But when she tried to undress you, you told her. Hands off, missy, I'm happily married!"

An 80 year old woman was arrested for shop lifting. When she went before the judge he asked her, "what did you steal?" She replied "A can of peaches"

The judge then asked her why she had stolen the can of peaches, and she replied that she was hungry. The judge then asked her how many peaches were in the can. She replied "6".

The judge said "Then I will give you 6 days in jail."

Before the judge could conclude the trial, the woman's husband spoke ….and asked the judge if he could say something. The judge said "what is it?

The husband said "She also stole a can of peas".

Morris is on his deathbed. He asked his nurse to be a witness to his will. His wife, his daughter and two sons are at his bedside. "So" he says to them: "Bobby, I want you to take the Beverly Houses. Tammy, take the apartments over in Los Angeles Plaza.

Steve, I want you to take the offices over in City Center"

Then he turned to his wife. "Sarah, my dear wife, please take all the residential buildings downtown".

The nurse is just blown away by all this, and as Morris slips away, she says, "Mrs. Smith, your husband must have been such a hardworking man to have accumulated all this property."

Sarah replies, "Property? The asshole had a paper round!"

The old man placed an order for one hamburger, French fries and drink. He unwrapped the plain burger and carefully cut it in half, placing one half in front of his wife. He then carefully counted out the French fries dividing them into two piles and neatly placed one pile in front of his wife. He took a sip of the drink, his wife took a sip and then set the cup down between them. As he began to eat his few bites of hamburger, the people around them were looking over and whispering. Obviously they ere thinking "That poor old couple, all they can afford is one meal for the two of them".

As the man began to eat his fries a young man came to the table and politely offered to buy another meal for the old couple. The old man said, they were just fine – they were used to sharing everything. People closer to the table noticed the little old lady hadn't eaten a bite. She sat there watching her husband eat and occasionally taking turns sipping the drink. Again the young man came over and begged them to let him buy another meal for them. This time the old woman said "No thank you, we are used to sharing everything." Finally, as the old man finished and was wiping his face neatly with the napkin the young man again came over to the little old lady who had yet to eat a single bite of food and asked "What is it you are waiting for"?

She answered – "The teeth!"

Bert feared his wife Peg wasn't hearing as well as she used to and thought she might need a hearing aid. Not quite sure how to approach her, he called the family doctor to discuss the problem. The doctor told him there is a simple informal test the husband could perform to give the doctor a better idea about her hearing loss. Here's what you do, said the doctor, stand about 40 feet away from her, and in a normal conversations peaking tone see if she hears you. If not, go 30 feet, then 20 feet, and so on until you a get a response. That evening, the wife is in the kitchen cooking dinner, and he was in the den. He says to himself, "I am about 40 feet away, lets see what happens. Then in a normal tone he asks, "Honey what's for dinner? No response. So the husband moves closer to the kitchen, about 30 feet from his wife and repeats, Peg, what's for dinner? Still no response. Next he moves into the dining room where he is about 20 feet from his wife and asks, Honey, what's for dinner? Again he gets no response. So he walks up to the kitchen door, about 10 feet away. Honey what's for dinner?.....

Finally she turns around: "For goodness sake, Bert, for the fifth time CHICKEN!"

At the regular Saturday morning service, the rabbi announce that he was planning to leave for a larger congregation that would pay him more. There is a hush in the congregation. No one wants him to leave because he is so popular. Fred Silverstein, who owns several car dealership in Newton and Brooklyn stands up and proclaims "If the rabbi stays, I will provide him with a new Cadillac every single year and his wife with a Honda mini-van to transport their children. The congregation sighs in appreciation and applauds. Saul Cohen, a successful businessman and lawyer, stands and says "If the rabbi will stay on here, I'll personally double his salary and establish a foundation to guarantee a free college education for his children! More sighs and loud applause. Estelle Rubin age 72, stands and announces with a smile, "if the rabbi stays I will give him sex! There is total silence. The rabbi, blushing ask her "Ms. Rubin, you're a wonderful and holy lady, whatever possessed you to say that? Estelle's 80 year old husband, Jacob is now trying to hide, holding his forehead with the palm of his hand and shaking his head from side to side while his wife replies. "Well I just asked my husband how we could help and he said F**k him"…

Chapter VII

Stories that Live Writes

The Pitcher Plant

To my mind, the life of a cat is no less precious than that of a human being.
- I Mahatma

One morning last spring, when I opened the door to pick up Barry's newspaper, thrown every morning at our front door, I found a dead bird lying on the porch. It looked deliberately placed there.

"Barry, come down, look, I think our cat Mika did this."

My husband, who was still in his bathrobe, made a face and said coolly, "That's nature, we must not interfere."

"But it's dangerous."

"A dead bird? Why?"

"That bird might carry diseases. Mika will bring them right into our house."

"I agree, but it is your cat and she's always up to something bizarre."

I shrugged my shoulders. "What does that mean?"

"That the cat is a nuisance."

I shook my head. At the time I didn't know how prophetic this statement would be.

Aside from his frequent bad moods, Barry's a role model for our family. He's a successful businessman, has his own private club membership, and is an admirable gardener. Our back garden has all sorts of plants, trees, bushes and God knows what else. Anyway, in summer we love to sit on the terrace and admire everything that is blooming there while getting slowly hammered drinking Bordeaux and bourbon.

That was the case at the beginning of June last year. The two of us, Barry and I, sat and had a glass of wine. Barry smoked a probably expensive Havana, and we were calm and happy as we looked at the flowers, or rather at his miracle, an exotic yellow-green giant plant with an aroma that was quite odd if you got too close to it.

"Don't worry, love", Barry said. "This plant can't harm you."

"I don't trust it", I responded.

"Who are you kidding?" Barry sat in his favorite canvas chair, with a cigar dangling from his fingers, half smiling at this huge bushy plant with a pitcher hanging from it like a rotten cucumber.

"Does it spoil your cocktail hour?"

"No", I said. "We are finally having a quiet Sunday afternoon in our garden."

"Do you know how large these things grow?

"Don't know 12, 13 feet maybe."

"Let me tell you it is actually a killer plant", he said half-jokingly.

I stared at my glass of Bordeaux on the table. I didn't want a sip but took one anyway and shook my head in disgust. "Why are you saying this?"

"Because I believe your cat has been trying to climb up that plant."

"God forbid", I said, "Mika's just wandering around it."

"And so was that garden rat, remember?"

"I don't like it. Why not just cut it down?"

Barry inhaled the cigar smoke deeply. "I'll think about it."

Suddenly he laughed. "You know, I don't really care about the cat. I am more worried about you."

Now I had to chuckle: "You know, that plant would have real trouble taking on someone my size."

Barry spat on the terrace. "We'll see."

"You really think the cat could have jumped into it?"

"Well, she always brings dead animals to our front door. She has to be finding them somewhere."

"She hasn't done it much during the last few weeks." Barry stood up. "Could be that small animals are disappearing in it."

"Because it is a pitcher plant, everything that falls into it gets eaten."

"More like digested".

"Barry, I feel like there is something you want to tell me."

"Well," he said, pulling another cigar out of his pocket. "One day I discovered that the plant looked kind of flat and dull. The trumpet hung down, almost touching the ground, so I investigated. I found there were no more insects in it, almost no liquid inside. The plant was dying."

"And then what happened?

2Well, that same day we had another dead bird at our front door."

"Right."

"Well, I took that bird and threw it into the pitcher. Two days later the plant was fine. It was looking healthy and seemed to have even grown a bit.

"So, what has this to do with anything?"

"The next morning, I saw the cat just wandering around the plant. That's it."

"She probably smelled the dead bird", I said.

"Probably. But a little while later the cat was gone and I investigated the plant. I looked inside but couldn't see anything, so I shook it a little. Suddenly, some terrible creature jumped right out of the trumpet. It looked like a huge pink rat." Barry paused a moment scratching his chin.

"A rat? How gross!"

"I think it might have been Mika. I think the liquid had dissolved her fur, so she looked more like a rat. She tried to run but didn't get far."

"How did you come to that conclusion today?", I asked.

"Because I picked the rat up and threw it back into the pitcher plant. Only days later I realized, we never found dead birds on our front porch again."

The Wrong Plane

Inventors don't have time for married life
- Nicola Tesla

"How did you get on this plane?" the flight attendant barks rudely, shoving the boarding pass in my face.

"Through the gateway, of course, like everyone else," I snapped, instantly annoyed.

One of the "air-waitresses" — as I call those creatures — drew a breath to respond but was thankfully interrupted by the pilot's announcement, *"Boarding complete, prepare for take-off."*

Overhearing our exchange and anticipating a scene, one of the male flight attendants nearby intervened and told her to step back.

Furious, she shot me a look so vile; if looks could kill, I'd have died on the spot.

Little did I know the matter wasn't over.

"So, where are you headed?" asked my extra-large, super laid-back seatmate, wearing the ugliest pink shirt I had ever seen. Of course, as a woman in her prime, I'm familiar with flirtation, particularly on flights.

"Barcelona," I replied, forcing a smile, "for a short cultural visit."

"Right… so first Johannesburg, then back to Spain? That's a long journey," he said.

I narrowed my eyes, my pulse quickening: "Johannesburg? That's not in Spain, is it?"

He paused for a few seconds, looking concerned, "Didn't the flight attendant tell you? This flight is heading to South Africa."

With my anxiety level rising, I realized why the "air waitress" had a problem with my presence on the plane.

In shock, I quickly dug out my boarding pass. And there it was — *Departure: London Heathrow, Arrival: Johannesburg South Africa*

"Oh my God!" I yelled, my hands pressed to my face.

"Please try to calm down," my flight mate soothed, concerned, casually stroking my elbow.

I'm slowly getting to grips with myself from the throes of a profoundly severe panic attack. I take a deep breath, "So," I exhale, "The plane flies directly to South Africa?"

"As far as I know, yes."

"But don't we still have to fly over Spain?"

My flight mate grins suggestively. "I really don't want to make fun of your situation. Perhaps I could help you make the best of it?"

"You know what, you're absolutely right."

"I'm Cody", he stretched his hand out, "I'm a frequent flyer."

"I'm Debbi. So, tell me, what does one do in my situation? I need to know."

"Well, Debbi, I suggest we get some drinks, and I mean something much stronger than coffee."

It crossed my mind that Cody seemed like one of the "good guys", a rare commodity nowadays. We were getting comfortably cozy. Chatting and drinking Martinis — Martians, as Cody calls them — and letting him occasionally touch my arm. It turned out he was single and hadn't been in the company of a woman for a long time.

We ordered more *Martians* and continued chatting. I felt happy — should I not have felt more miserable given my predicament?

"We should get closer," Cody suggested.

I smiled, but not because of his remark. I suddenly had an idea, possibly the most elaborate I'd ever had. I whispered my plans into Cody's ear.

Cody, who by now smelled like a distillery, enthusiastically encouraged me, instantly agreeing to play his part.

Twenty minutes later, the flight details screen indicated it was almost time to execute the plan. We were now directly over Spain.

Cody saw it too, smiled, stroked my knee again, and whispered: "Here we go… and don't forget, 5000 and one night with you." I winked at him and reclined my seat completely.

Then everything happened at the speed of light.

"Help, we need help!" Cody shouted. The other passengers were startled by the commotion. At the same time, my "air-creature" began running up the aisle towards us.

"This woman is in insulin shock, Cody shouted.

"Looks like she's already in a coma."

The flight attendant crouched down in disbelief. "Is that foam coming out of her mouth?"

"Yes, said Cody. "Look, I'm a doctor. This woman already told me she's having an insulin episode — she's in shock now."

"We should move her to the rear," suggested the flight attendant, who had started to sweat profusely.

"No, there's no time to waste," Cody interrupted. "This is an emergency! She can die at any time. Please inform the captain immediately!"

Seconds later, the pilot announces, *"Ladies and gentlemen, we have a medical emergency and will begin our descent. Please return to your seats immediately and fasten your seatbelts."*

We all felt the sudden drop in altitude, and within minutes, we were on the ground.

"We've landed in Barcelona," Cody whispered.

It was like a typical chaotic medical drama scene from that point on. Medical staff flooded the plane and started moving me into the terminal on a stretcher.

I pretended to be unconscious, not an easy feat given the commotion.

Where was Cody? I needed a big strong guy by my side right now. I couldn't fool the Spanish doctors for much longer. Any second now, they would realize I was faking it.

But the act held out.

While the staff were distracted, I peeked just enough to realize I was lying parked in a hospital corridor. Now was my chance to escape.

So, like a thief in the night, I snuck out of Chaos Hospital, giddy with the realization that we had pulled it off! My plan worked, and I was exactly where I intended to be.

And that almost would be the end of the story if not for the Cody matter.

Honestly, I intended on keeping my promise to Cody to take another flight to South Africa, but maybe that would have been asking too much? At least, that's what I keep telling myself. But it's still on my mind, and who knows one day…

Flowers on the Wall

Never argue with a fool, onlookers may not be able to tell the difference
- Mark Twain

My husband says it's my fault I have jungle fever.

I wouldn't call it a fever exactly, but he has a point because we live in a jungle of sorts.

Last year we found our dream house on one of our Sunday walks. And it wasn't only the exterior of the home that turned out to be authentically historic.

The external bricks were very well preserved, and the entire property had a European air about it. Inside, you could walk from room to room via hidden doors, like in a castle.

It was the garlands, however, that made the house uniquely unforgettable. The home was even listed for historical reasons. We would never find a mansion like this again.

The previous owners had allowed the garlands to overgrow. So, as soon as we bought the house, I told Barry we should have them cut down because they could start attacking the brickwork. And Barry initially agreed with me.

The garden was also overrun by small palm trees and bushes planted by the previous owners. We needed a gardener right away and rushed to hire one on Craigslist.

A disaster was inevitable.

Barry was beside himself. "He's chopped everything down! The entire garden looks like a bulldozer ran over it!"

Every plant, every bush, had been cut at least three feet. It looked so abysmal that I almost cried.

"This fucking wetback has no brains!" Barry cursed. "He even cut the palm tree branches — how insane must you be?"

I shook my head. "Maybe he didn't understand your instructions."

Barry approached me, his face crimson with rage. "Is it my fault he doesn't speak English? What is there not to understand?"

I simply shrugged. "So now what? We need a new gardener, right darling?"

"Today!" Barry yelled. "And I promise you this — Nothing will ever be cut on this property again. *Ever!*"

I didn't know at the time how serious he was. I also didn't know that garlands grow faster in spring.

They were not simply growing; they looked like a green explosion in slow motion, having doubled in height and thickness within a month, from three feet high as they were when we moved in. Eventually, they grew all around the house, growing tremendously, covering even the windows.

It has since been a year, yesterday my sister came to visit.

"Oh my god!" she squealed as she stood in the doorway. "What happened?"

I smiled and realized then that you couldn't even see the street from here because of all the bushes, garlands, and weeds in the garden!

She stopped, stunned, in front of the door. "The house… your beautiful house looks like an ancient Roman ruin."

She didn't stay long either. She said that the garlands, some of which penetrated through even the most microscopic crack, made her anxiously uncomfortable. My sister, you see, always needs to feel safe or rather, she needs to be in a safe space.

I calmed her down and told her that even creepy fairytale forests have benefits. Barry couldn't help but laugh out loud.

That was yesterday afternoon. By that evening, our world looked completely different.

What happened, you're wondering? The ceiling in the bedroom collapsed! Fortunately, we were not in the room, but startled by the noise, we rushed over and were astounded to see the sky.

Even more astounding were the garlands growing wildly on slabs of roof tiles. I immediately ran to the phone.

"Are you calling the roofers?" Barry shouted after me.

"No," I replied, we need a new gardener!"

Faux Pas in the Restaurant

Even before I traveled to Japan, I heard that I'd have to change shoes if I go to the toilet. You can bring your own slippers or sandals, but most often, you can get a pair of slippers that are lying around at the toilet entrance.

But one night in Osaka, when I went to a nice traditional Japanese restaurant, I had to go to the toilet, but couldn't find any slippers near the toilet entrance .

I opened the toilet door and winked to my wife in the restaurant, asking her what to do. She said, "Don't worry, just take your shoes off."

That's what I did, and after using the toilet I walked back into the restaurant area.

When I arrived at the table my wife laughed out loud, but all the Japanese customers gave me a funny look.

Suddenly a waiter came from behind with a mop. I turned around, and I saw my own wet footprints on the polished floor.

On the way back from the toilet I had forgotten to put my socks and shoes on; and frankly, the man's toilet floor was very wet, which was of no surprise, considering that I had a bladder problem.

Vacation in Nature

Peggy's first serious fit of laughter began on the drive to Florida, where the whole aria started.

"We agreed there would be no drinking in the car," I said.

"Didn't you ask me what the whiskey bottle is for at the grocery store?" asked Peggy.

"Yeah."

"And what did I say?"

"For the road, but that doesn't mean drinking while I'm driving."

"Look out the window, honey." She pointed her finger forward. "That looks like a road to me." Peggy took another deep sip and unexpectedly started laughing.

"Disneyland 50 miles ahead," I said.

"I hope we find the amusement you promised me."

"You already seem amused enough."

"I haven't even started, and please stop picking on me." She took another sip.

But Peggy had a point. We were bickering back and forth on where to spend our vacation.

She said the Florida Keys, but I suggested Disneyworld — it would be so much fun, or so I thought.

In a nutshell, we spent only one night near Disneyland. Beyond that, even my free-spirited, open-minded Peggy could no longer stand the ridiculous bullshit ever created. Of course, Peggy was shocked and mad at me because Disney had been my idea again. So, we checked out of the mediocre hotel early, got in the car and discussed where the journey would take us next.

"No matter where we go next, I'll feel out of place," she said.

"Where do you want us to go?" I asked.

She took a deep breath. "Where are we headed now?"

"South."

"Alright then, let's keep going south."

"You want me to stay on the highway?" I ask.

"Whatever, I think the Keys are south."

"The Keys?"

She looked at me. "I am not talking about your door keys. I mean the Florida Keys."

"It was just an idea," I mutter.

"Okay, whatever, we're heading south."

"Not if I stay on this road."

"Why not?

"It goes straight into the Everglades."

There was silence for at least a minute. Then, "Hey honey," she said finally, "I think it might be fun there."

"In the Everglades?"

"Yeah, I mean, they got all kinds of animals there and real nature."

"If that's what you want, we'll go there."

"Of course," she replied, half smiling, "let me find a good place to stay."

"A log cabin would suffice," I said.

Later that night, we found a wonderful little place just at the park entrance.

Peggy said she felt better in this wooden enclosure than in our fleabag joint the night before. She said nature was making all the difference and that the Everglades is supposed to smell and sound like nature.

Anyway, the next day we were already on a boat. It was a small airboat, those typical Everglades type passenger vessels with a giant propeller.

It was exciting, windy, and the landscape consisted of mangroves, swamps, and grasslands as far as the eye could see, and the boat — or beast — as Peggy called it, was faster than a sprinting dog.

We looked at each other grinning — what an adventure, just the two of us and the skipper, whom we paid extra to be alone. A private adventure tour, so to speak. Then it all happened very fast. Smoke began to billow behind us, and then abruptly, the engine died.

The boat edged towards the shore, engulfed in acrid blue-grey smoke. "Hey, skip," I said to the driver, "what's happening?"

He didn't answer, and it looked like he tried to pull at something on the engine.

"Is there a problem?" I wanted to know.

The guy shook his head. "The engine leaks," he said.

"Meaning?"

He climbed down toward us. "Meaning, you have to take your stuff and get off the boat."

"And then what?" Peggy was beside herself.

"Then, we need to walk about ten miles to the park exit."

"Honey, get your phone and call for help," Peggy instructs.

I touched her shoulder lightly, bracing myself. "I left it in the car."

Her eyes widened. "What! You don't have your phone... seriously?"

As expected, she was livid.

She turned to the driver, "Can't *you* call someone?"

He shook his head. "I am sorry, batteries are low."

"You got to be kidding," Peggy shouted. "First, the boat leaks, and now the batteries are low. I'd hate to see what..." She continued her rant.

The driver managed to bring the boat to shore using an enormous stick as an oar and then quickly stomped straight into the bushes like he knew the way.

"Can we make it before dark?"

"I am afraid we'd need to camp for the night."

"Do we have a tent?" Peggy asked.

As it were, evening fell rapidly while we were lying somewhere in the Everglades in the middle of a small island of sand and grass. But at least we had the fire the guy made.

"Honey," Peggy said. "Something's moving there… behind you."

I looked around. Something dark and long moved through the grass.

"Just a Python. It won't harm you," the guide said.

Lost for words, I saw Peggy grip both hands over her mouth like a vice.

Not a minute later, we heard dull croaks getting closer; it sounded like an old man belching nearby.

I hugged Peggy and pulled her to me. "Look there in the water on the stick… something's crawling."

"My God, what is that?"

"A bullfrog," I said

"No behind the stick!"

A dark, sinister-looking shape moved silently through the water, stealthily approaching without causing any noticeable movement. "Alligator!" Peggy shrieked.

"You got that right," the driver said. "I suggest you guys move away from the shore right away."

Peggy jumped back at lightning speed just as I heard a loud splash.

Peggy shrieked again, even louder than before if that were possible.

"The alligator just ate that frog," I said.

"I can't do this anymore, honey, I just can't," Peggy started to cry.

We all tried our best to sleep that night lying around a small fire, and as if everything else wasn't enough, the mosquitos were relentless. Finally, maybe about an hour before sunrise, Peggy fell asleep in my lap.

The following day, we walked for maybe an hour when suddenly Peggy began to cry tears of joy as an exit path came into view.

Of course, we cut our vacation short after that, although, in hindsight, it had been an incomparable adventure of a lifetime. Our homecoming, however, wasn't the end.

We received a letter from the Everglades boat rental company about a month later. It was a formal letter of apology and something else in the envelope. A cheque — of a very substantial amount — was made out in our names. Nothing to be sneezed at, for sure.

"That just made my day," Peggy said.

"That's great news, but just wait a minute."

"What's wrong?"

"I think there's a catch. Look at the cheque."

Peggy took it, *"Only Redeemable at the South Florida Commercial Bank Everglades City,"* she read aloud. "That's strange."

I shook my head. "Means we'd have to go back there."

"Well," she said, "I think that the sum on that cheque is well worth another trip."

"As long as we don't rent a boat."

"Don't even mention the word," she said.

And then we were back in the car heading south. This time, on the way, we both had a laughing fit —we were laughing all the way to the bank.

Amnesia

Do I really believe I had amnesia? Depends on the day.

I have been accused of a horrible crime, one that that happened at the station. As I entered my home, witnesses claimed they saw a middle-aged woman with me. The cops had a warrant, and her blood was found in my bathroom.

I remember the interviews with the cops most clearly, b but from the beginning, I insisted had I never met the woman. They insisted too, but then again, I can't say, because I have a medical certificate which shows without a doubt that I suffer from amnesia. It shows that I'm incapable of committing a crime.

One of the cops actually looked like I'd drawn sympathy, justified sympathy, because there's no doubt that I'm the poorest SOB they've ever seen in their career. And I have to admit, they treated me like a human.

"You may have amnesia, but we need to know, do you know this woman?" the young, pale-faced cop asked.

I said, "Okay, it's true I have amnesia, but of course I remember Laura."

"What else do you know?"

I shook my head. "No memory."

The big one looked at me coldly. "We don't have a warrant for nothing. Blood was found in the house."

"So, am I accused of murder? That's awesome!"

"So that's it? You'll have a murder charge coming up."

"Amnesia is not insanity; I need a lawyer since I don't know anything."

The two stared at me for a few seconds. "I highly recommend not playing games with us," the old bastard said.

"I swear, Sir."

"Do you have travel plans?"

"No Sir."

"Okay, we have your statement. That's it, so far."

I shook my head. "Sir, my amnesia is really getting worse, so I have to go into town. I need to go to the hospital."

"Don't skip town, mister."

I sighed and turned to the young one. "Listen, is there a way I can borrow a hundred dollars somewhere? For the taxi, you know. I'll pay you guys back."

The two police officers looked at each other as if they had just seen Bigfoot, and the young man shakes his head and rummages through his pocket for cash.

"You'd better get there now," he said, not even looking at me.

I thanked him.

About a week later, at 9 o'clock sharp, someone knocks on my door. This time, it's only the old fat policeman from the station.

He said he needed a second statement and wanted to go back into my house, so I let him in and let him sit in the kitchen.

"So, you need a written statement?"

He nodded as if expecting something. I guessed right, and I went to the kitchen cupboard and rummaged around for money like it was my piggy bank. I slipped him two hundred dollars in silence.

"For the young fellow, from last week, sir."

"Tell me again. When was the last time you saw Laura?"

I explained to him as best I could. I told him Laura wanted to move on, start a new life,

"...I have her address too," I said concerningly. "She moved to Seattle about 6 months ago for a new job."

The fat cop crossed his arms. "Her parents filed a missing person report, and you're still the only connection we have to Laura."

"And they think something happened to Laura."

"You got that one right, boy."

"I'm sure she's fine," I reply defiantly. "The fact that I'm a suspect has something to do with my neighbor who blackmailed me."

"I understand, but as you know, you have an old rap sheet."

I brush it off. "Nah, ancient history."

"Old or not, we wouldn't have considered you if you hadn't previously been charged with attempted murder."
"I was acquitted!"
"Just like the rape trial."
"I was nineteen then!"

The old fat man shakes his head. "Where is she? Give us a clue and we're good."

"I have to look for a note. She wrote it down by hand on a piece of paper. Give me some time."

His eyes seemed to pierce me. "If I don't hear from you by tonight, you can't afford bail, guaranteed."

Around five in the afternoon, I picked up the phone. I said I just got back from the doctor, and I have a new report. Unfortunately, I still have severe amnesia, and I'm really sorry, but I can't find Laura's note.

His voice deepened: "We're almost on our way, buddy," he hung up.

Something had to happen soon, took the detective's business card and wrote an email. I really forgot where she lives, but I am going to Seattle first thing in the morning to try to find her and solve that case myself.

Minutes later, I received a reply. *You have 48 hours.*

I thought for a moment and then wrote: *I guarantee that I will find Laura, and I will be back. But to guarantee you this, may I ask you to take care of a little thing? You will find what I mean in the attachment.*

The headline of the attachment read: *Will pay back more*, and the file was my hospital bill of 900 dollars.

Days later I found out the bill was paid. And as far as I remember, I am still in Seattle.

The Young and the Old Bear

A young bear is slowly reaching marriageable age.
Father Bear says to him, "So that we don't make fools of
ourselves, you practice on a knothole first, my boy."
The young bear steams off, looks for a hole in a branch and
practices vigorously. After two hours, he comes back and
says he is now perfectly prepared. The old bear agrees and
gets a female bear. He asks the youngster to try out what he
has learned with the female bear. The young bear goes after
the lady bear, takes a long swing with his leg and kicks her in
the butt with all his might.
The old bear is horrified: "what are you doing?"
The young bear cooly says: "first I had to make sure there are
no bees in it."

Five Stars in Colombia

Our next trip as a semi-retired teacher and small family —
being only my daughter and me, took us to Bogota,
Colombia. After all, my credo so far has been "travel should
also educate". Not only because of a lack of money for
popular tourist destinations but also to occasionally escape
the semi-functioning bubble my country had become.
Although looking back, I believe I now have a much clearer
idea of what semi-functioning really means.

Anyway, my daughter Mathilda convinced me that
Colombia was safe and that five days would bring about a
much-needed quantum leap in her language skills. In any
case, I find South America intriguing. Still, I'm a realist, so I
insisted on full travel insurance because I believe in safety
first, which is my other credo.

I had already found the city in the world atlas. Bogota.
Despite being a vast city, it had a limited number of decent
hotels. Somehow, from what we could gather from the
reviews, many looked substandard or plain ugly.

We're looking for the best deal and notice that even the
famous, expensive hotels seemed highly overrated.

Mathilda suggested we try lesser-known booking sites. Finally, Mathilda found a fantastic deal. The famous 5-Star Sheraton, at an unbelievable price.

Two weeks later, it really happened. Airport and first impression, first class. However, the taxi ride left much to be desired. The vehicle looked like the tiniest yellow taxi in existence. The driver, who bore a striking resemblance to a Venezuelan dictator, understood zero English. And the music, which was cranked to the max by a loudly screaming woman, didn't help us feel any better either. (As we found out later, these noisy singing women are, in reality, men, and the disease is called Vallenato).

We were shocked when we finally arrived at the legendary Sheraton. A dark, stark concrete apartment building stood pitifully on a pot-holed street in the Chapinero neighborhood. We were startled to be greeted by two overweight, horizontal-trade women at the entrance. Then we saw it, *5-Star* stuck to the thick glass door, enormously large and made of wood. But as soon as I got to the front desk, I realized that this hotel had to be a mistake. The guy at the cash register rushed to summon someone who spoke at least a little English making it clear that the "Big Sheraton" was somehow different. Luckily, it only took ten minutes of back-and-forth, and a few hands and feet, for him to understand we had booked for five days and already paid for it.

The rooms were spacious anyway, and the staff tried their best. However, the following day things started to change. We discovered fat cockroaches in the bathroom and the closets were black from dust and dirt. I immediately contacted my travel insurance, but unfortunately, they don't pay for dirty rooms or overrated hotels. My daughter had an idea, however. She took pictures of the closets and cockroaches and asked for diarrhoea medication at a nearby pharmacy. Then, I contacted the insurance company again. I informed them that we had become ill due to poor room sanitation and hygiene standards sending photos of the medication and the receipt. A few weeks later, the insurance refunded our stay, and Mathilda had improved her Spanish.

The Swimming Pool

"We won," my wife Maggy informed me this morning, knocking on the bathroom door.

"You mean against those tourists?"

"Yes love, Old Glory showed them!"

I immediately clenched my fists and grinned into the mirror because our well-earned vacation could finally begin. Maggy said she thinks the other tourists in the hotel were all from Eastern Europe. Admittedly, my wife had even more resentment than I did for these types of tourists. So why do I feel this way toward Eastern Europeans?

I googled Eastern Europe the day before and showed Maggy an online map to ensure she knew where the planet's dark side was. She said she'd already been there and driven to a country called Czechia. Still, it may as well have been Chechnya because Maggy confuses things at times.

Anyhow, until last week we were in Spain, south of Europe, I think, and honestly, it was the first time we'd crossed the pond. If I were to go overseas, I'd always said it would be London, my dream country. However, we ended up in Spain because, at the time, Maggy was about to start a diet.

And because Spain was known for its healthy, garlic and red wine-loaded 'Mediterranean Diet' style food, it was a fitting choice.

A positive, of course, was our hotel — excellent, with a balcony and pool. Maybe a touch crowded, but by all standards, fantastic. There was a nightclub downstairs, and Maggi loved to dance, alone on the dance floor, rarely with me, and rarer still with strange, stifling Eastern European men wearing white socks.

Did I mention our room came with a balcony directly over the pool area? Fantastic!

The nightmare began when we went to the pool, where we usually went first thing after breakfast.

But when we arrived, we were taken aback when we saw that most canvas chairs had already been occupied.

And I have to admit. It got worse. I discovered that some guests had pre-reserved the chairs the night before with their towels.

By the seventh day, I was exasperated. Barely before most guests had finished brushing their teeth, all the chairs and sun loungers were already taken by those Eastern Europeans' big butts or towels.

So, I ran red-faced down the stairs and rushed straight to the pool area that morning.

I approached the nearest two lard buckets sleeping spread-eagled on their sun loungers. They'd been snoring there since at least sunrise.

"Excuse me," I said.

No reaction. "Hey, wake up... *get up*!" I yelled.

They looked up, incredibly annoyed and sloth-like, lifting their ugly asses almost in tandem.

They stared at me and mumbled in strangely sounding Russian... or could have been Spanish. Anyway, I had my say.

"Hey, you've been occupying all the chairs with your towels before sunrise for a week now," I said.

They both screwed up their faces as if they'd smelled a skunk. At the same time, the woman pointed her fat thumb towards the reception while the guy kept mumbling incomprehensively before laying his fat ass back to sleep.

"What the hell!" I said.

She replied something unintelligible, making no sense.

But I wasn't done with them yet — that much was certain.

The following morning my wife woke me up at 6 am sharp. "Darling, I hear the foreigners marching," she informed me.

"I'm ready," I said.

I went out to the balcony and saw them trotting along — an army of vulgar, ignorant hooligans.

But I came prepared. I grabbed a giant Old Glory towel covered in stars and stripes with both hands. And, as the Russians or whatever they are, were about to sit down, I threw the towel over the balcony, directly onto the double sun lounger, hitting it dead on! You should have heard those folks protesting en-masse.

Fur and Skin

Some say I'm terminally ill; others think I'm just a curiosity. Anyways, I try hard not to take myself too seriously, and frankly, I consider myself an abbreviation of nature. After all these years, I got used to my own reflection somewhat, and actually, at times, I can even laugh at my face. Depends on the day.

And to be clear, I don't feel incapacitated at all. So let me spit it out: what I have is a disease called hypertrichosis, which is an abnormal amount of hair growth over the body and face. In short, you have hypertrichosis if you look like a fur-covered ape.

I am not going to lie to you. I don't have to, and fact is, at the moment I'm living with my mother, who will be ninety next week and looks two generations healthier than me, which of course is superficial, because remember, it's only what's on the inside that counts. My mother always says I am beautiful, and as it turns out, for some, I actually am.

However, there are times when I feel stricken because of my appearance, and while I am not a shrink, I admit that I also feel unsettled at times when I am excluded. So forget all these little wannabe victim-princesses. Yes, that's me, the victim in the corner, still kicking and screaming.

Anyway, my friends are right when they say I need to make more of an effort to finally find a suitable woman. Right across our building on the ground floor lives a beautiful big woman. It seems she is Hispanic, with her smooth hairless skin and dark, meaningful eyes. The truth is, she would be the ideal person for me, a dream come true. However, the problem is, she probably already has a boyfriend, unless he is just an uncle or relative who lives with her. He's an ugly bald man with a mustache, his arms full of tattoos. I know he is abusing her, and I assume he is a mean, dirtbag drug dealer.

Of course, she knows my face. She has to, because am famous around here, and she greets my politely, sometimes even smiling at me when we bump into each other on the street or at the convenience store around the corner. That's how I know she loves potato chips with bean dip and Jell-O.

Actually, she's the one who starts small talk, really just chit-chat, nothing important at all, but she pays attention to me, and she nods kindly when we depart, although I am not sure if she is only befriending me out of pity.

Then came the big incident that destroyed pretty much everything, what a mess it was!

It actually started with a good idea. Did I mention that I actually find my body appealing in a certain way? As an animal lover, I appreciate everything dark, everything covered, where black hair covers the pink skin. Anyhow, it all accumulated the evening before Christmas, and God was it a mighty cold afternoon. It's hard to believe, but I actually own a fur coat.

I was waiting for the woman. She came home at dusk, and we met right at the stairs in front of the house entrance. I implemented my plan right there. Voila, I opened the fur coat with both hands and for three seconds, she was fully exposed to my true nature, just as God had created me. At about the fourth second, a maddened scream echoed through the night.

Needless to say, all hell really broke loose after that. The police knocked on my door, a day later, the psychiatrists followed.

Frankly, I had to start all over again, and that was the main reason I've moved to a new place. It's been over two years now, and nobody would believe where I ended up.

I now live in a green, tropical country of 17000 islands, here in exotic Indonesia, far away from civilization, right in a jungle village. Under God, I tied the knot with a local. Yes, I actually did get married. To make the story short, I became a curiosity, or even a local celebrity. My wife, just like the girl from the old neighborhood, has those meaningful eyes, outer and inner beauty, and the same disease I have. Of course, people call us names, as we are the two village Orang Outangs. No worries, it doesn't affect us, and we are stars! We even have far away friends and followers sending us tons of donations!

The House of Excitement

"So, are you serious about getting your own massage parlor?" big Jenni asked.

"Oh dear," Laura, her best friend and caretaker of her baby said. "You have   been trying for years, why are you still insisting?"

"Because I'm *this* close." Jenni put her thumbs and forefingers together.

"What's missing?"

"The license, of course. Then I'm done."

"And then?"

"What do you mean then? Then I'll open my own shop."

"You're in Vegas."

"I know that."

"You can't pull something like this off here alone."

"That's what the woman from the massage school said too."

"You can't work independently, right?"

Jenni nods, concerned. "Yeah, I need help."

"You also need financial help."

Jenni got up and walked to the kitchen counter and pulled a cigarette out of a metal can. "And that's the biggest problem."

"Don't count on the banks."

Jenni waved her hand. "Never, but I've still got an ace up my sleeve."

"What's that?"

"My Uncle Joe from Texas. He's coming to Vegas next week on a business trip."

"That could be your ticket."

Jenni's eyes shone. "I know he will. Believe me, a few minutes with him and I'll be all right."

"So, is this going to happen?"

Big Jenni agreed.

And as it turned out, Uncle Joe agreed, but he wanted 25 percent of the business, and he would hand over the cash only a little at a time. That, of course, was a nightmare in the making, but as beggars can't be choosers, Jenni accepted.

From the moment we first rented the space in a bungalow-type home near Henderson, the restoration of the space was a slow and, at times painful process.

And then big Jenny was ready. She was standing at the front door with her legs slightly apart, smiling almost in circles. She was wearing pink sports panties and a bright blue sleeveless shirt.

"Welcome, everyone, to our pre-opening sessions," she shouted.

"You've got to be a good provider," a young guy with a red baseball cap said.

"Hey, the girls you got in there are all Chinese?" a bystander about double the size of big Jenni asked.

"Well guys," Jenni said, "what you see is what you get."

"What does that mean?" somebody asked.
"It's all about me. I am your willing masseuse," Jenni said, half laughing.
"So we have to take quick turns for 30 bucks, right?"
"For 20 minutes, darling. Opening special."

And so it went on, and the guys took their turns. Most of them enjoyed it, or at least, they officially said so. On social media, the establishment gained its reliable reputation rather quickly, although a few people bitterly complained about the lack of quality and esthetical issues that, for some at least, were related to big Jenni.

It would have almost been all milk and honey for Jenni if it weren't for her pushy uncle, whose lack of commitment made it almost impossible financially for an expansion of the parlor, including furniture and staff.

And every time he was in the area, he demanded a special massage from Jenni in his hotel, but Jenni took it rather lightheartedly. At least, it seemed that way.

On the contrary, Joe got pissed off at every little thing, every dime he spent too much, and his own wet dreams of the still nonexistent staff.

The peace lasted only a short while. Actually, until one evening when he showed up unannounced at the parlor and rudely kicked out a customer to see Jenni.

"Here you are again," he said. "You're trying to do everything yourself!"

"How dare you, Joe!"

"*Me*? How dare *I*?"

"You're coming here, throwing a customer out?"

"I needed to speak to you. In person."

Jenni remained flabbergasted for a moment. "I have to tell you something."

"I am here for a reason," Joe said. "We agreed that I would get a monthly payout."

"After your investment," Jenni responded angrily.

"Look around, Jenni. Does this look like nothing?"

"We need staff, we need massage table, and we need doors, not curtains."

"You said that, but I need to see if this place makes money."

"I need cash to make cash, Joe."

"Anything else?"

"Yes, there is. We have to do some advertising."

"For what? You already have customers."

"Let me tell you, if I hire staff, we'll need to advertise it to get folks in here."

Joe shook his head. "Like a grand opening?"

"Like a huge grand opening, with a press release and a couple of vloggers for livestreaming, those kinds of things."

"Okay, you got me, and I'll bring my buddies."

Jenni had to grin. "Okay, you're forgiven, but we need to get started."

"How much?"

Jenni told him.

It took Joe another month to cough up the money, but then it all came together quickly: The official, long awaited grand opening.

Two Chinese and black beauties from the Caribbean made the team. Jenni dropped colorful balloons on the waiting crowd from the roof.

The dozen or so guests who were waiting hoped that the day would be a great new beginning. No more sneaking in into a half-legal enterprise with no guaranteed happy ending.

And indeed, Joe and his business friends, or who cares who they really were, showed up in droves.

Standing with her legs wide apart and her fists on her hips, Jenny announced: "Welcome guys, today we have a welcome deal. You get an all-inclusive oil massage for 10 minutes for 20 bucks. How does that sound?"

The guys stormed into the building, bumping into each other. Some were even cursing their way in.

"A great day for you Jenni," Joe said.

"Yeah, we're good. A few things, though."

"Like what?"

"We still don't have fixed doors in the rooms."

"That's nothing," Joe said. "Curtains will do the job, we're all good."

"And no advertising. Not enough funds, Joe."

"Look at the all the people. It's gonna be great!"

"I hope so. If the higher power gives us a great day."

Jenni points her finger to the sky.

"What do you mean? We're good, right?"

"Look at the clouds!"

"Damn, looks like a storm is coming up."

"Highly unusual for Nevada in winter."

"Well, it depends."

Ten minutes later, the first thunder cracked and the wind began to blow. First you see palm trees moving a bit, but that was only the beginning. There was a crack of lightning, and the doors slammed, flying open and shut.

And then they screamed.

Men cursed. Suddenly, the door flies in a high arc towards the parking lot. Most men waiting outside had to run to their cars, but some, the most desperate and barely of legal age, were still staying outside, stubbornly waiting for their tun.

For some reason, some started to laugh. They were peeking through the open entrance.

What they saw was sheer chaos. The curtains had been lifted up by the wind, and at least three men tried to put on their underpants at the same time, but the wind was stronger than the toughest men. They stood helplessly naked in the hallway, and God be a witness, some even showed signs of recent over-excitement.

"The greatest show on earth," a youngster screamed from outside.

"Fuck off," a customer shouted.

Jenni started to panic, but Joes grabbed her shoulder, preventing her from running. He yelled at her against the wind.

"Don't worry about nothing, Jenni. This is a fantastic thing. You'll be all over the internet. It'll be the best advertising ever!"

One Veterinarian

"Starbucks and environmentalist veterinarians fit together like Faust and Liberace," my colleague, the incredibly intellectual skinny-like-a-scarecrow Candida Clarkson says.

"So now you're an expert on sounds and literature?" I say, intending to sound ironic, but it gets lost on her — stupidity, the culprit.

"No, not at all," she says, smiling. "I was wondering why meet here? Why not rather wait at the office for him?"

"I suggested Starbucks because the rookie, George, is new in town and wanted to meet up after his first day at work."

"Sure, that explains it," Candida says. "Because you needed to close the office a little early."

I shake my head. "Not early, just punctual; remember the heat we got last time when we worked overtime?"

"So you closed at six?"

"Well, the glass door upfront, I thought it was appropriate to close it fifteen minutes before official closing time."

"Just like the tax office."

"Just like… you know," I say, nodding my head in the direction of her privates below.

Candida stares out the window, where it gets dark and rainy. "You know, I consider the newbies as colleagues too."

The door opens, and our improbably tall red-headed, barely twenty-year-old rookie, George Hamilton, strolls towards our table.

"There comes the rookie star," I say.

We grinned as he sat down.

"Thanks for meeting me," he says, sounding oddly disturbed.

"Any problems," I ask.

He shakes his head. "Not really. A bit unusual, perhaps."

"Well, it was your first day in the fields. How was it?" Candida wants to know.

He shakes his head, grinning sheepishly and looking slightly embarrassed. "I can't even say."

"You can tell us anything; we're your colleagues," Candida insists.

"Alright then," he says. "So this morning, I went to a farm, but I only met the farmer's old grandmother when I got there." So, I greeted her and told her I'm a veterinarian and supposedly there to inseminate one of the cows."

"Yes, my boy, come with me... I'll show you." She tells me.

Then she led me to the cowshed, and, pointing at one of the cows, she told me, "Okay, my boy, the cow is over there, and you can hang your pants on the hook right up here."

In Paradise

Paradise. I love that word. Paradise can be everything or just one thing. But staring at the sparkling, blindingly reflective surface of the swimming pool - how else can I describe it? Paradise!

I lie on my canvas chair, stare at the shimmering water, and occasionally take notes with a simple notebook and pencil. This year, before my end of year retirement, the manuscript for my autobiography has to be ready.

I repeatedly start from the beginning, at least in my head - Was it a good life, or will it be a good life?

Regardless, I'm sitting comfortably here on the hotel terrace, and the pool extends right up to the fence where the beach begins. There aren't too many people around me. How much better can life get?

So far, the sea is calm, with hardly any wind - even the heat is still bearable.

Right by the shoreline, just behind the surf, something dark is flailing in the water.

Relatively large, but too small to be a beached whale.

Curiosity gets the better of me. I get up and slowly walk towards the beach. I stop a good twenty yards in front of the dark form. Does it smell slightly rotten?

Yes, it must be a seal, but that's unusual because you usually find them further north. Maybe the seal is injured?

I slowly approach the dark mass. That's not a seal! Impossible. It's not even a whale. An octopus, perhaps? Too dark. God forbid - is it a corpse? I feel a sense of panic rising in me. I rub my eyes and kneel at a distance of maybe ten feet from the mysterious dark form.

The middle of the body is black and smooth; however, the tail-end is undoubtedly too long for a seal.

But the face is the most unusual feature. What does it resemble, then? It can't possibly be - it has human-like features!

I leap up and jump back. The creature has the face of an ancient woman - oil-smeared with hair slickly pressed to her head. The eyes, however, are entirely black, more like a gorilla's eyes with no white showing at all. The creature blinks, and I am both terrified and intrigued. Now, its mouth is moving, and it hisses, much like a cockroach, only louder. That's impossible… Slowly I take a few steps back, and then

I run, faster than ever before in my life! I jump over the fence back to the hotel, run up the stairs, and only come to a stop in the bedroom, where my wife lies on the king-size bed focused on her laptop.

"Jonny, what happened? You look like you've seen a ghost!"

I double over and rest my hands on my knees from exhaustion. "Down on the beach," I gasp, "there's a strange creature! At first, I thought it was a dead seal or whale, but it's not!"

Jenny puts the computer aside and adjusts her glasses. "And what was so strange about it?"

"It had a human face."

She pauses a few seconds. "Jonny, a dead animal can have all kinds of features, even facial features, especially when it decays."

"This one is different. Let me have your camera - I have to take pictures of it!"

"It's in my handbag. Go ahead, I will meet you there in a few minutes."

I am running back, thinking this is the craziest thing I have ever encountered. But I'm sure Jenny's right... she has to be right!

The mysterious creature is still flailing in the sand. Carefully I get closer.

I need to take perfect pictures, especially of its face.

Suddenly it begins to whisper something. "Come closer... come closer." The thought that I'd gone mad shot through my head, but I distinctly heard those words.

I move my head closer to the creature's head. The dark eyes are, in fact, those of a gorilla; this thing is real!

"Come closer... come closer." It whispers continuously. Suddenly I feel dizzy. Then – darkness.

I'm waking up in a hospital room. Jenny is sitting next to me, pale as a sheet. "You had passed out. I found you on the beach."
I could barely get a word out. "The creature?" I whispered.

Jenny shook her head. "There was nothing, Jonny. But, for now, you need to recover first, and the doctors have to examine you again completely."

Months later, we had long since returned to our everyday routine. The vacation and the incident were almost forgotten when Jenny called me into our shared home office one evening. "You remember that thing you found on the beach?"

"How can I forget? That thing was so real!"

Jenny points her finger at the computer screen. "There seem to be more of these. Judging by this article, someone else found something similar too. In fact, many of them at once."

"Let me see." I'm narrowing my eyes slightly, and what I see is even more bizarre. "That looks like three or four of them!"

"And they're smaller, like babies."

"But the same type of creature, right?"

"Zoom in, check out the facial features. "

I click and flinch. "The faces... my God!"

Jenny nodded, deeply concerned. "You see it, right? They all have a resemblance to your face. They look like a hybrid of something or someone."

"Related to me?"

"Jonny, they found you with your pants down, so what exactly happened there on the beach that day?"

The Inventor

I have a solid retirement. Having been a teacher in a public commercial school for almost fifteen years, I'm in a better position than most. After all, nothing is given these days and I'm grateful for that. I still have a lot of adventure-spirit in my middle-aged bones, and my wife, who still teaches in an ordinary high school, agrees.

Furthermore, I always do a pretty good job of telling my wife the truth about my future plans. She sticks to me like glue, except for if she suspects something unusual regarding former female colleagues and special friends.

Anyway, I have to stay focused. My idea is to start a business, not so much for the money but just to show that I can do something else besides teaching.

So I teamed up with an old friend who has an inventor. Marry says she likes the idea, mainly because she thinks my strength was explaining the business model. After all, it had all the elements of a teacher-student relationship. The business even included homework.

Admittedly, my alleged strength as an explainer didn't quite work out at first. I had no luck at the bank with financing, though I had been a customer there for twenty years, and although Marry has always been cheerful, this time she really laughed when I presented her with my financial plan. But then she agreed partially. Why not present this business idea to a group of former colleagues? She'd also invite her colleagues to a private teachers' evening.

A week later, all was set up and the party could start. They were all sitting in our living room like innocent sheep, ready for the next step.

"I'm sure I've never introduced you to my husband Jack," Marry opened the conversation. "Jack is present tonight, and we have prepared something for you that will change your life."

Colleague Meyer leaned his neck all the way back. "Please, no lectures on Buddhism," he said, half-joking.

Marry clasped her hands in delight. "Much better. The best husband in the world, my Jacky has a small business model that he would like to introduce to you."
What a great opening, I thought.

"Come on, Jacky, let's get started." I fixed my tie, took the portable white board and placed it right in front of the pundits.

"I am glad so many of you have come. That makes this easier," I said.

They stared at me silently, and suddenly my breath caught, and I felt blood rushing up my throat.

"Are you nervous?" a Blonde asked curiously.

I cleared my throat. "I'm here to ask for twenty thousand dollars for five percent of our company."

Silence. "Company?" Interrupted the big guy in the lumberjack shirt. "Since when you guys have a company?"

"Well, we're not there yet," I said defiantly, "but we'll have a real company soon, with accountants and all."

A murmur went through the living room. Marry pressed her hand over her mouth, probably because she was laughing.

I cleared my throat again. "Well, I'm standing here humbly in front of you to offer you a historical business opportunity. We have a business package, and we need all of you on board."

An elderly woman looked at her watch. "We would appreciate it if you can let us know your business in due time."

"Of course!" I pulled out a marker and drew a large black rectangle on the whiteboard, writing *world map* underneath.

"This is a new card," I announced. "It gives you cash back after your routine purchases."

"How much do I get back?" the Blonde interrupted.

"Well, it depends, but up to 30 percent."

"Not gonna happen," someone shouted.

I tried to smile. "You just sign up, and retailers get a commission."

"I don't understand anything you say," said the guy in the lumberjack shirt. "I sign up, and then what?"

The Blonde pointed a finger at me. "And then you want us to sign other people up, right?"

"…And I don't make any money if someone signs up underneath me," the old granny said.

"Yes, you do," I said loudly. "You get your return as soon as you find your four directs."

Again, the Blonde interrupted. "Hey, just hold on, can you finish this analogy?" She raised her hands and closed the triangle above her head. "So up there it's you. Then underneath it's us," She spread her arms. "And then at the bottom is the bottom line, and everybody I bring in, they bring in."

Now I had to interrupt: "Yes, correct, and now it's getting bigger and bigger and bigger."

She smiled. "What shape am I making here?" She closed her hand with a wide move, like a triangle, or better yet, like a pyramid.

People talked at once, and they were all somewhere between excited and agitated.

"Calm down folks, everything will be fine," I shouted. "We've got everything secured on paper. Marry, can you please give every guest a form?"

Silently, Marry handed each teacher a sign-up form. An old woman tried to get up.

"You cannot leave," I said aloud.

"Or what?" A big guy asked. "Are you expecting to sign us up to invest in this?"

"Are you threatening us?" the Blonde asked.

Suddenly, my wife said: "If you don t invest today, you won't hear about it again tomorrow."

"Excuse us?" The Blonde was getting angry.

Marry smiled. "I say this because I'm leaving my position at the school, and I'll become an independent business owner. So, if you're planning on making a lot of money before you retire, let's all do it together."

"Marry, what's that?" the old granny asked. "Are you seriously supporting this? Where did you get it?"

"What did I just say? If you don't invest today...?"

"Exactly."

Marry was half laughing. "I believe Charles Schwab said that."

"Oh, then it is serious," the big guy shouted. "They've got Schwab investment on board, is that right?"

I pointed my finger at him. "You've got that one right." I took a deep breath. "Of course, you can leave. But if you want to be part of one of the biggest investments in history, just sign the paper. I promise you it's going to be a surprise."

"From teacher to teacher," My wife added.

Most of the folks signed up that evening. And the truth is, we made enough money to move to Florida just a few months later, never to return to that old life.

The Hunting

We are newlyweds, married since June, and we moved to the rugged countryside to achieve our goal of living a self-sufficient lifestyle. We both work online, and honestly, we prefer to keep to ourselves, given today's climate.

However, just a few weeks after we moved into our retreat, grave differences of opinion emerged.

Sue didn't know that hunting would be necessary for our daily meals, let alone that I was an experienced hunter.

During the first two weeks, she vehemently opposed any kind of hunting. Until that is, she saw the steaming pot of mouth-watering stew on the dinner table one evening. Then, conceding to the merits of hunting, she suddenly wanted to be a part of my next hunting expedition, begging me to come along on a hunt.

I was about to gut the wild boar in the shed when Sue sneaked up behind me.

"What are you doing with the head?" she asked.

"I don't know yet." I pressed the hacksaw to the animal's exposed neck and focused on the task.

"I could make soup with it."

I shook my head. "If it were bigger, I would mount it on our wall."

"Will you go hunting again soon?"

"As a matter of fact, I will. There's a herd of deer roaming around nearby that I'd like to hunt."

"Please can I come with you, please?" she begged again.

I began to skin the animal. "Okay, no problem," I said. "But you need to learn a few things first."

"Like what?"

"Well, at least the basics of how to hunt."

"Yeah, I'd like that," she said, pleased.

We talked longer, and Sue again eagerly wanted to know every detail. So, finally, relenting, I promised to take her to the forest tomorrow.

It was a particularly dark morning, but we were ready. First, I showed Sue how the gun worked. Then, explained that when you've shot an animal, it's important to claim it immediately after shooting because anyone nearby can and will claim ownership of it. Often, the animal will belong to whoever reaches the carcass first.

Sue seemed overly confident that she understood everything. "Be careful," I advised; sometimes, other hunters roam the area."

"Harry, I need to confess something."

"What's that?"

"I don't know much about animals. You said we're hunting deer, right?"

"Right."

"What do they look like?"

"Like in the movie Bambi, only bigger."

"How big?"

I shrugged. "It depends. Some can get as big as a horse."

She nodded confidently again. "I'm sure I'll make a good hunter."

"I hope so," I said. "For everyone's sake."

After a two-hour walk, we reached a ravine from which we could see a broad field. And there, behind some bushes, we saw a decent-sized stag that we couldn't see before. Carefully we crept closer. I motioned for Sue to sneak up behind the animal. I must confess; she looked impressively professional as she stalked the animal, gun poised.

A few seconds later, I heard a gunshot. I raced over to check that Sue did everything right. As I approached, I could see Sue and a stranger standing over the dead animal, arguing wildly. Then, I heard the stranger say wearily, "Okay, lady, whatever… It's your damn deer if you say so. But can I at least take my saddle with me?"

The Upper Crust

As I sit here established, I make to write something on white paper when my aunt suddenly calls the family to dinner.

Quickly and yet with composure, I make my way to the dining room, where they're all already seated. Uncle, aunt, my father, and a bit incongruously in a lumberjack shirt, my husband-to-be, Daniel.

On the table are two porcelain candlesticks with lit candles, appetizers, and probably the best wine in the house sits on the table, ready to be served, everything as it should be in a decent mansion household. For Daniel, it is his first time here in my family's inner circle, on my side of the aisle. All old money, as he mentioned before, and probably will mention it again. It's a point I really don't want to go into detail about now, otherwise I'll get sick before the feast even starts.

Smiling innocently, I sit down, and the upcoming family topic of conversation is already set: Daniel and I are engaged, and today we are supposed to make it official. Of course, the upcoming explanations are already waiting as well.

Daniel had already started to help himself to the food when my aunt whispered into my ear with a fake smile: "Your future husband still has to complete a short behavior course if he wants to be part of our family."

I make a face as she says, "…and you have to tell him that today."

The tormenting family conversation develops in a similar awkward way, except my dad is beaming from both cheeks. He seemed to like Daniel from the get-go for unknown reasons. But for the other folks here, Daniel is as abhorrent as a rat in the basement, considering he sells mattresses for a living. Plus, he has already gotten my dad involved in a business, or a sort of business, so to speak. This is another topic I'm trying to avoid at all costs, but it happens anyway.

"That business," my uncle Joe says, "will never work. Nobody wants to join a pyramid scheme." He smiles towards Daniel. "Besides, don't you think that it's a little inappropriate for us? Take a look around."

Daniel grins. "That's only because he is not doing his downline. We just got started."

My dad keeps silent and keeps staring at the wine.

"He will make money. Fresh, well-deserved money," Daniel adds.

"Never," Uncle Joe says. "He has enough of his own, he just agreed to it out of politeness."

My aunt finally interjects as politely as she can. "We won't talk about that tonight, and we will all behave."

"Because I will explain that we are engaged," I say.

"Exactly," Daniel smiles at me, "and remember, you shouldn't be ashamed of your husband."

As expected, the rest of the evening doesn't go too smoothly, so I urge Daniel to shorten the meal. I just want to get out of here.

"Daniel and I want to do a little sightseeing trip before it gets dark," I say truthfully.

"Then let me accompany you," announces my mother.

Daniel and I have no choice but to agree, as long as she's sitting in the back seat of the car.

I whisper to him to avoid any conversation with my mother while driving.

Before we get into the car, my mother still gives her comment. "You know, darling, before I give my traditional consent to your cohabitation with Daniel, I want to make sure *he* can behave outside of our four walls as well."

"I beg you, mother," I protest in a small voice, "he really can."

So, we pulled off in Dad's shiny sedan and slowly drove away. We roll slowly down the avenue, and as Daniel drives, he is as silent as a grave. So far, so good. The next traffic light turns red, nothing unusual, except for a black Lincoln that also stops next to us. An elderly, apparently well-heeled lady looks curiously into our window.

Suddenly, Daniel rolls down the window and sticks his head out. The woman from that limousine also rolls down the window and smiles at him.

Daniel smiles right back and says, "Well, did you fart too?" He seems to say something else under his breath as well.

The woman seems to get upset. "You called me 'old cow'? How dare you?" she says.

"No ma'am," Daniel says. "I am not judging people by their looks." Then he babbles something incomprehensible to her, and it almost looks like flirting.

For some reason, the woman in the other car seems to be smiling, and she makes a movement with her finger.

Then suddenly my mother starts to yell. "That's it, Daniel! Leave the car. My daughter and I are returning home. Get out!"

And that's exactly what happens. Daniel gets out, gets in the other car, and drives off with the unknown lady. Luckily, I never hear from him again.

The Weird Spanish

German pensioner couple, Fritz and Eva, are considering renting an apartment in Spain, preferably for the entire summer. However, it's risky because they don't speak Spanish.

It's essential for Fritz that the apartment is quiet since he does not want to be disturbed. Nevertheless, the two pensioners are tech-savvy and manage to rent an apartment on the island of Mallorca online.

When they finally arrive in Spain, they find their apartment is in a locally populated residential area — without a trace of another tourist.

Children are shouting and playing everywhere, and music blares from the neighbor's open window.

"What do we do now?" Eva asks her husband.

"Now it's rest time. I'm drained from the trip and need sleep for a couple of hours."

Eva looked worried, "With all this activity and commotion, it will be impossible."

The two pensioners are exhausted and want to rest but realize they have a problem because they don't speak Spanish.

"I've thought about it," says Fritz. "I've thought of a Spanish word for *to rest,* and I'm going to tell the neighbors, especially the kids, that we want to rest now."

"Good luck. I've also thought of some Spanish words if you need help, by the way."

Fritz addressed the neighbors and kids, and when he returned, he said everything was sorted out.

Ten minutes later, there was knocking on the doors and windows. When Fritz opened the door, he found the neighbors, kids and even parents on his doorstep. Everyone was jubilant and festive, and the kids brought a music player.

"Fritz… what's happening? What have you told everyone?"

"I told them it's rest time."

"Isn't that called *siesta* in Spanish?"

"I said *fiesta.*" Fritz shrugged, going red in the face.

The Experiment

At school, Sandra asks her classmates: "Is it true that old people smell different?"

Her friend Gabi replies, "Well, they all smell rotten."

John laughs. "No, only the dead are rotten. Old people are not dead yet. They are still alive."

Gabi chuckles. "All right. Then we will call them mature. But as a matter of fact, I don't care how we call old people. I just don't want to be near them. "

John raises his hand. "Wait a minute. I once saw an experiment on YouTube. It shows that old people don't smell any different. Scientists let three groups of people sleep in shirts: old, middle-aged, and young. Each person had to sleep in the same shirt for five nights, and the shirts were not washed. Then they asked volunteers to smell the shirts. The volunteers didn't know which shirt came from what group, but all agreed said that the shirts of the old people smelled the best."

"What kind of volunteers were these people who want to smell old people's shirts?" asks Sandra.

John: "They were, of course, old retirees."

The Cheese Stinks from all Sides

Harold Johnson had fallen in love. For a few weeks now, he has had a new girlfriend. He met her at the library, a mature, intellectual woman with attractive inner qualities. He told her he was a pensioner, and she told him she worked mornings at the farmer's market cheese stand.

Mr. Johnson had plenty of free time in the afternoons, so he spent most of it in the library.

He and the woman shared a common passion. They both loved to read classic literature and cookbooks in the library. Recently, he invited the woman over for a glass of wine and kickstarted their relationship.

However, the relationship was not without its problems. Mr Johnson had a severe aversion to her scent. Frankly, her smell made him nauseous. So he bluntly told her that she smelled like blue cheese, and as a result, after every visit, his entire house stank.

She reasoned that the smell must have come from somewhere else as it would be impossible to drag a cheese smell over long distances.

But then she confessed to lying about having a job at the cheese stand when they first met because she felt embarrassed that she was unemployed.

Mr. Johnson was relieved to hear that and confessed that, in reality, he was not a pensioner as he'd said before.

Still, the mystery remained. Mr. Johnson couldn't understand why she always smelled like blue cheese.
"So, what do you really do?" he asks her.

"I'm unemployed but volunteer at the Foot Disease Clinic, changing dressings in the Fungal Infections Treatment ward."
"I guess that explains the smell," Mr. Johnson remarked.
"So then, what do you do for a living?" she asked.

"I work on a farm in the pig stalls, but fortunately only in the morning."

The Winning Ticket

I was sitting in my bar, which is not that unusual since I consider myself an afternoon drinker. Then, suddenly, the door opened, and my nephew and his friend hurriedly approached me.

"You're not going to believe it," my nephew says, trying to impress me.

"What is it," I say.

"Uncle Larry won the jackpot!"

I shake my head, unimpressed. "Nah, he doesn't even win a beer at Bennigans."

"I swear!" The boy points to his goofy friend, who seems to be freezing. "This is Mickey, Uncle Larry's stepson."

I give him a friendly nod. "Hey kid, how's it going?"

"Just fine, Mr. Jones."

"Call me Jimmy, so your dad won, huh? What did he play?"

"The Powerball."

"Nice," I try to smile. "So he won big, like what, six numbers?"

The boy shrugs. "I suppose he did. I heard he bought himself a yacht."

"Is that right? How do you know that?"

"An asset broker came to our house, wanted to talk to my dad. That's how I found out."

"Hey J," my nephew says. "I can go down to Fort Lauderdale and check things out."

I thought for a second. "You know what. We'll go together."

"That's great, J."

"Let's find this motherfucker. Your uncle owes me."

A minute later, we all hop into my Ram. On the way, I explain to the boys that Uncle Larry owes 100 grand worth of debt to our family.

We arrive just before midnight. The old shotgun house looked unchanged outside, with stray dogs and garbage everywhere.

"I bet he's hiding the stash someplace near that dumpster," I remark.

"How are we going to handle him?" my nephew asks.

"We always start by being polite," I say.

"And what if he doesn't want to pay?"

"We keep being polite until it's time not to be."

"Look, his car is still there. So, he must be in the house."

"That ain't his car," I say, squinting and pointing my finger at the strange old vehicle in the dark.

"I think he's got something."

"Like what?" I ask.

"It's too dark, but it looks like an old-timer, a classic."

"He always had peculiar tastes," I say.

We don't want to waste any more time and decide to pay him a visit right away. As he opens the door, the smell of crusty old beer mugs hits us.

At first, he tries to argue but then confesses that he never won the lottery. He had bragged that he did, just to show off. I am not convinced. I demand my money either way. Finally, after a heated exchange, he gave me the car keys. The car did little to put a dent in the debts, however. I continued to glare at him. Then, very slowly, he handed me his lottery ticket to check if it was worth anything. As it turned out, it was typical uncle Larry — big sinner, no winner.

It Happened in China

Every time my husband Tanner and I argue, we try to laugh it off within an hour. In short, we turn our arguments into jokes. For example, he claims he's the world's best husband, and I point out his faults. Recently, however, he's developed a worrying, frequently occurring problem where he becomes disoriented, yet he jokes about it.

There have been situations and places where things took unexpected turns. For instance, when we were in China recently, there were days when he believed we were in Washington DC. There is no clear explanation for why this happens to him, but he likes to claim it's from our constant arguing.

Another example was on this trip. Because it was cheaper than a taxi, we took the train a few times to get around and explore our surroundings. On one occasion, while waiting for the train, it happened again.

First, he criticized me for sitting on the train station floor. I particularly enjoy sitting on the ground and find the position comfortable and not in any way unusual. But, within an instant, he morphed into a chauvinist pig. He barked at me to stand up because he believed sitting on the floor looked terrible and I had no manners.

"Tanner," I said with a scathing look, "I don't need your advice. And honestly, your manners and ideas are archaic, so do me a favor and stop acting so macho."

"Women should know their place," he mumbled under his breath.

"I heard that!" I snapped. "I'm warning you, Tanner, if you make a scene right now, I will walk away and leave you ranting to yourself like a lunatic." And once again, I reminded him that he married a modern feminist who wouldn't put up with his chauvinistic nonsense."

Increasingly agitated, he begins to escalate. "Leave then, you old twat!" he shouted, "go on, see if I care."

The world seemed to fall apart for him at that moment. In an instant, he became so irrational that I believe he had a severe panic attack or memory fugue. But honestly, I don't really know what's wrong with him.

Suddenly he sputtered words unintelligibly. However, judging by the locals' expressions waiting for the train, he seemed to be speaking perfect Mandarin.

Then, he walked around and turned to a local man squatting on the floor. What happened next is unbelievable, but it happened. In a tirade of mixed languages, he ordered the young Chinese man to get up, gesticulating wildly with his hands, which is extremely rude and culturally inappropriate in China.

"You are in China, and in this country, we squat," the man replied in surprisingly good English.

Mercifully, nothing more happened, but Tanner can be so damn arrogant. That same evening he called the airline, but just before making the call, he informed me.

"You're right", he said. "We are in China, and you did what the Chinese do... I forgot the rest of what you said today though." And with that, he made the call to the airline and later that night, we were heading back to Washington.

Spies

"We are targeting the old granny with the white beard, that's the enemy" said my Uncle Joe, my sponsor and self-acclaimed neighborhood vigilante. He slowly put his binoculars down, snatched a cigarette out of his shirt, and lit it without taking his eyes from the kitchen window across the old building on the other side of the street.

We're both good observers. We have to be, because the old man across the street isn't the old grandfather most of us always believed. He is, as it turns out, a pervert.

The other truth is, Uncle Joe is not my real uncle, but just someone who cares, and I'm a currently unemployed graduate student living with my uncle and mother. We've been observing this man for weeks, and since yesterday, almost around the clock with binoculars. Because originally my half-sister made a scary observation, which is what started the whole ordeal.

At first, we thought the guy was just being rude, or judging by the evidence, that he was treating his significantly other badly.

I adjust the sights. Nothing to see. "Do you think anything else will happen today, J?"

He leans against the wall, inhales deeply. "It's still a bit early, but we'll catch him."

"What exactly are we going to do if we catch him?"

"First, taking pics. The more embarrassing, the better."

"You want to blackmail him?"

"Who said that?" I could hear his slight annoyance. "Once we have the photos we confront him, let's see how he reacts."

"Are we good for now?"

"Hey, keep your eyes on him, I think something's moving over there."

I immediately zoomed in. "I see something colored, red and yellow; it's moving up and down!"

"Can you see all the windows?"

Good point, that obviously requires some skill. The old condo on the other side of the golf pond, about 200 yards above the golf clubhouse, is on the 3rd floor. However, the view of 3 windows of the condo was okay. Strictly speaking, we had a good view into the bedroom, expecting the pervert to make a move.

"They've caught him a few times before," my uncle says. "Always with colored hair."

"I've got the camera ready," I say.

"When your vision is clear, take lots of photos in quick succession."

"Working on it, J."

I actually manage to get some good shots, because the display showed there was lots of colorful hair. But what he did exactly remained a mystery to me.

Back in the car I asked again. "J, I know you don't tell me everything. What exactly did the guy do, and what should we do with the photos?"

Uncle Joe lights another cigarette. "Let me tell you a story. And keep the window closed, okay?"

"I know the draft is killing you, J."

"Well, if that motherfucker didn't have a penchant for colorful wigs, we might

have just shrugged our shoulders even if we knew his sexual preferences."

"Does he clean himself with wigs?"

Joe coughed and laughed at the same time. "First of all, the guy is no stranger to your sister..."

"Half-sister," I interrupt.

"Anyway, she wanted to know what her true love is really like. Maybe he's a criminal or has an affair with someone, so she hired me."

"And what do we know? He's playing with wigs?"

"Wigs also play a role, but that fag got himself a doll. Not just an inflatable sex-doll, but a totally realistic dead-gorgeous love-doll. Unbelievable. He almost fooled your sister. But we won't snitch, because a doll is not a person!"

"Sure," I say.

"Show me the pics," he says.

And there it is. That couldn't be a person, and if it wasn't, then it must have been a replica of a human.

He looks at me as if he's seen a ghost. "To good to be true," he says.

"So, are we snitching?"

He shakes his head and smiles. "There's no need."

"What do you mean?"

"We may not have caught him cheating, but there's a market for this stuff online. We can make some serious money here."

My Secret Suffering

"Mr. Jones, while we found that you have low blood pressure and anxiety, we also have an explanation for your panic attacks. But none of this is life-threatening."

And so ended my first doctor's visit in many decades. But I knew that was only half the truth because the disease was undeniably deep inside me. So, what's wrong with me?

Susi says she believes me when I insist that I feel the end is near.

"What should I do with my remaining time?" I ask her.

"Darling, try doing something worthwhile, something you will be remembered for."

"Yeah… you're right," I say. "Although writing a book or creating a painting would take me forever."

"Write short stories darling. You used to do that when you were young and dashing."

Why hadn't I thought about that? What a great idea. I probably have enough time for short stories, so I could try my hand at that again. I nod decisively. "That's exactly what I'm going to do. In fact, I think I already have some script ready."

As it were, less than a few weeks later, my first short story was published, with a promise to readers of a sequel. Of course, I wouldn't benefit from this, but that wasn't the point. Readers enjoyed my story so much that they began contacting me directly, urging me to write more and turn the stories into a series.

It didn't take long before I gained more readership and fans from my short story series. The trick to my success is always offering sequels. Fuck, can you believe it? Even the doctor has become a fan.

Anyway, success or failure. Secretly, I'm just glad to be alive.

I still feel ill, but no one knows what I have specifically.

I'm getting myself admitted to the hospital as a precaution, concerned that this may be my last trip. I look at my wife. "My darling, everything has an end," I said pragmatically.

She shakes her head. "No, Barry, the sausage has two. And it's not over yet."

I was in the hospital now, and from what the doctor said, I would have a definitive diagnosis by tomorrow. That evening I felt terrible and almost fell into a coma. Pre-emptively, with the last of my strength, I requested a specialist physician. Not twenty minutes later, he's standing next to my hospital bed. He greets me with a chuckle. "Very pleased to meet you; I'm your biggest fan."

"You enjoy my short stories?" I ask.

"You bet. I can't wait for the next one to be released."

"So, what's the final diagnosis?"

He shakes his head. "I'm truly sorry —"

"Doc," I interrupt. "Be honest with me… how much time do I have left?"

"Very well," he says. "Let me put it this way then — if I were you, I wouldn't start a new short story for the series."

The Pastor

"See that man in front of the chair waving his hands?" I asked my wife.

Susy stretched her neck. "The one who looks like a mafioso?"

"That's our new pastor."

"Probably a good choice for our renovated Parish."

And that was our first impression of a true character. Yes, our little Parish has been renovated. It was a former bar that had been freshly painted in a nice burgundy, and the new decorations were pure and clean without any ridiculous church ornaments. Somehow, this ominous new pastor from New York fit in with the new decorations. Oddly, when we first met him, he also wore a burgundy-colored shirt with dark blazer and polished burgundy shoes. With his jet-black hair, he had more than a little resemblance to an old Mafioso, and considering his unknown past, the only difference between him and a real gangster was that he hopefully had already made peace with God and himself.

Today was the first mass in our community church after the renovation, and we could hardly wait to hear what our new pastor had to say.

"I'm curious about what he has in store for us as a newcomer," Susy said in a slightly critical voice.

And then he started, and it appeared from the beginning that the new pastor was kind of a charming fellow, though. He talked in a low voice, smiling quite often, and he spoke about redemption, about a new life that will await anyone if they keep an open mind, and most people seemed kind of impressed. Susy said it was pretty good for an otherwise boring Sunday morning. At the end of the sermon, he said: "I think many of you are here in attendance, but let me tell the truth, some of you—and if you are honest, you must agree—not all of you are true believers."

There was a murmur in the hall.

At the end of the speech, he walked around, handing out pamphlets.

He told us that we were all cordially invited to a special meeting the next Friday to explore faith and steadfastness and to advance spiritually. To be honest, I agreed with him, and I already accepted it in my own mind. I filled the paper out right there on the bench, and we both signed up. After all, I found him to be brilliant, a man with new ideas, a new broom, so to speak, and later, according to the chatter in the parking lot, some elderly fellows were quite captivated by Pastor Michael's speech.

However, it turned out, we had a lot more to chew on than we originally thought, because the following Friday, the mix of attendees were totally different. There were a lot of younger people, and I saw some obvious single mothers with their young children, some who looked like they were looking for something, some kind of redemption.

And there he was, our little mafioso-turned-pastor, again in his burgundy and black outfit.

His speech was warm and inviting, but by the end of it, his tone and message changed somewhat when he began speaking about the apocalypse.

His voice echoed off the walls: "The end is near. Are you ready to give up everything for Him? He who will set you free, who will forgive you for all that you and your brothers and sisters have done wrong for the last two thousand years? And are you now ready to renounce your sins?"

Yeah! came out from over a hundred throats at once.

"Now, are you ready?" his voice rose in pitch, and he raised his fist: "Are you truly ready, right here, right now, to receive HIS blessings?"

Yes! echoed loudly through the hall.

"...Now and today, the gates of happiness and eternal blessings will open to you!"

People were standing up, the entire hall cheered, and for some, tears of joy began to flow.

He raised his voice again: "Do you want total happiness, total liberation, here and now?"

"Yeah!" it echoed. "Yes we want it," a high-pitched voice screamed.

By now, everyone was standing. They were one crowd, excited with desire and ecstasy.

Then, two girls appeared in white robes. They wore small rosaries on their heads, and one stood to the left of Pastor Michael, the other on his right. They stretched their arms forward, and both held onto an oversized copper chalice. They smiled while Pastor Michael looked around with a serious look, checking if his words were sinking in, if they were ready. Silence. There was a click from behind, and I turned around. A third girl was fumbling at the front door.

"They locked us in," I whispered to Susy. Everybody just stared at the pastor, like an enchanted crowd that was frozen in time.

Slowly, the pastor raised his voice again. "And now take this goblet, this holy cup of the Lord, which will bring you all true love and true deliverance from every misery imaginable!"
Solemn organ music sounded from somewhere, then the girls stepped down from the podium and approached the crowd from each side of the aisle.

The goblet was handed to everyone present with a friendly smile. I could not believe it; each and every one of those people took a sip from the goblet.

The elderly couple next to us did the same, and they even smiled gratefully at him.

Then they reached Susy. She had already taken the thing in her hands when, for some unfathomable reason, I put my hand between the goblet and her mouth at the last second. I didn't know what was going on, and I grabbed her arm and pulled her up and to the exit. And there she was still standing, the little white witch, still trying to close the door with a huge key. I didn't hesitate in pushing that stupid thing aside. Light, fresh air. We were outside. After that, I don't remember much. Was it darkness or deep sleep? I was home. In any case, all hell broke loose that night.

When we heard the ambulances that night, it turned out to be a convoy of ambulances, the fire brigade, and the police, all driving right past our house towards the Parish. We knew immediately that something impossible had happened. We didn't hesitate for a second, thinking we could maybe still help our friends there. We both jumped into the car and drove back to the Parish, but already in the parking lot, I saw chaos.

Ambulances and police cars lit up the night. Paramedics with stretchers ran madly into the church, and when I looked at the dark asphalt, bodies were lying everywhere, some poorly covered with cloths, others scattered across the compound, police still sealing everything off. I knelt down and buried my head in my hands. They all had been poisoned. Why did he do that? How could such a tragedy happen?

"Harry," Susy sobbed. "Look, the faces, the faces of the dead."

"Please don't look at their grimaces, Susy. It's just rigor mortis."

"No Harry, please look again. It really is true. All the faces, they're smiling. They're all smiling."

Adventures in the Spa

Mr. Hooker is a restaurant owner and a chef, he owns a small restaurant at a railway station and sells fish and chips there. He has many regular customers because most of his guests are working-class people who like his nondescript simple dishes.

In the after-work hours he frequently goes to a spa that's run by attractive female employees just to calm down and relax. Actually, it is a complete spa facility that includes a soaking pool and Turkish bath, a private place that's perfect for relaxing away a long day.

Some time ago Mr. Hooker went again to the sauna. That day the temperature of the herbal sauna seemed to be especially high. Mr. Hooker had already been seating and sweating on the sauna bench, when the door opened.

A man came in and Mr. Hooker recognised him immediately. He was a customer.

However, he didn't like this particular customer, knowing his *disgusting and obnoxious table manners, besides he suspected the man being a politician.* But most importantly, the customer had denounced him once, because he was of the opinion that the restaurant was dirty and selling liquor without a license.

The other man also recognized Mr. Hooker.

The man smiled: "Good evening, Mr. Hooker how are you?"

Mr. Hooker *looked up in disgust* and disbelief. "So far, everything is well."

"Sweating cleans the body." said the man.

Mr. Hooker shook his head, he had enough for the day and left the sauna.

After a long shower Mr. Hooker went into the changing room, a big room with many lockers. The towels were hanging on a hook. As he toweled himself, the thought the towel was wet but it didn't matter, and *he only wanted to get out of there.*

 Mr. Hooker *couldn't believe his eyes* when he finally reached the exit.

The client, he met in the sauna, was standing outside on the door.

The man looked at Mr. Hooker and smiled: "Excuse me, but you have used and taken my towel!"

Mr. Hooker shook his head. "No, I don't think so."

"Please have a look in your bag." said the man.

Mr. Hooker opened his bag and pulled a towel out.

The other man still smiled. "Now look here, in the corner of the towel I have written some letters, my name actually."

Mr. Hooker held the towel close to his eyes and said:

"Are you really the most hated man in British history?"

"That's me, Tony B." said the man.

Mr. Hooker gave the towel back to the man. *Actually, he never returned to the* spa.

The Real Pollock

Recently my wife's brother told me he had bought a Jackson Pollock oil painting at a flea market. But I didn't believe it for a second and let her know. Yet, Jenny said she vouches for him and says he's an honest skin, eccentric maybe, but an artist for sure.

"Even if he has found one at a flea market," I say, concerned, "your brother is too poor to own a real Pollock. Besides, a painting like that would need to be insured and locked in a safe."

Jenny shrugs her shoulders. "Maybe so. But you know my brother always finds things at flea markets."

"I think he's in over his head. He lives on a boat because he can't afford a house."

Jenny picked up her wine glass looking annoyed. "I disagree," she says. "Living on a boat doesn't make a person poor, and there's a marina with a strong community and lots of artists there."

I smile, probably a little goadingly. "That still doesn't explain how your brother could ever find such an exclusive painting — and in a flea market of all places, no less. Nah, he's nuts, we know that."

Jenny pauses for a moment. "How much do you think a Pollock is worth?"

"Millions, at least."

"Oh my God," Jenny started to giggle.

"If it's an original," I say.

"So, how can we know for sure?"

"Tell your brother we'd like to come over to look at the painting."

"But you don't know much about art, do you?"

"I think I do. I mean, maybe I can give him an estimate or —"

"*Or*," she interrupts, "you could write a nice article about him and his discovery."

"Possibly... I do work for a newspaper, but a story like that could go two ways," I say.

"Oh whatever, darling, if it goes the wrong way, it makes you a great sensationalist!"

"Maybe so, but your brother won't be pleased with what I'd have to write about him and that likely-fake painting."

"Oh," Jenny smiled broadly. "I wouldn't be too sure about that."

The next evening, we boarded his boat. I'm taken aback. From what I remember, it looked like an old trawler, but the guy seemed to have a talent for renovations.

George seems jovial as he greets us and waves us into the cabin.

I was speechless. I expected to see a boat cabin, conventional with benches, wooden tables, and low ceilings. This ceiling, however, seemed noticeably lower. The entire floor space was buried under at least a foot of junk, including hundreds of used canvases and vintage garbage-looking antiques. "This must be your working room," I said, stating the obvious.

"I know it looks chaotic," George says, "but I actually work here."

"What's that smell? Maybe you should open some hatches?"

"I'd rather not; I don't want the salty air getting inside."

Jenny shouts from somewhere on the port side before joining us on the boat. "Darling, be careful not to get dirt on your new clothes."

I nodded impatiently, cautiously balancing each step across the unsteady dumpster-like floor. No need to get messed up for a stupid article.

"Alright," I say. "So, you have a famous Pollock painting?"

"Sure I have," he says.

"C'mon," I say conspiratorially, "Did you paint something you're now trying to sell as a Pollock?"

"Of course not! I might be a painter, but I'm also a collector."

"What do we have here?" I ask, staring at something ancient, what looked like a hideous old master painting, perhaps centuries old? I held it close to my face. "This is an ugly old painting, truly revolting, don't you think so?"

"This one?" he points his finger directly at the surface. "This is an old Venetian mirror you're looking at."

I realise the guy's right, remembering I haven't shaved in days. What a shame, anyway, shit happens.

Jenny has her camera ready and wants to make a video.

Finally, he points to the alleged Jackson Pollock original, a vast canvas full of colorful paint splashes.

"That's right," I remark, "he painted such shit. But, honestly, I'm unimpressed. It looks just a few decades old, and it's just paint splotched haphazardly on a canvas."

My brother-in-law remains calm, he says he compared the picture with all the other Pollocks, so it must be authentic.

I shake my head. "And you expect me to believe that and write an article that you have an original Pollok here?"

"It might be a bit dull and dusty, but it's an original Jackson Pollok, signed and dated." Then he pointed to a small painting standing next to it that looked fresh, full of red and yellow bright spots. "And this," he says, I just painted myself to see the difference."

"You have talent," I say, impressed by the painter standing next to me. Mesmerised, I sat down, wanting to take my time admiring his work. "I wish I could take these gorgeous colors home with me!"

"Well, your wish has come true," George remarks. "You've just sat on my color palette. So, if I were you, I'd write a good article about me and the Pollok, unless you want your new rainbow jeans going viral on YouTube."

The following Sunday, an article in the Sun Sentenial newspaper appeared:

New Jackson Pollock Discovered - Surprise art found on an old trawler catches marina community off guard!

A Young Man's Journey of No Return

"Barry, I'm really concerned our son may be retarded. He's supposed to pass his high school diploma soon, but…" Mother Jones shakes her head, concerned, "…well it doesn't look good."

I put the newspaper aside for a moment and adjusted my glasses. "His math is not that bad, and he's a good thinker."

"The other day, the teacher called me," the mother says, "telling me that Daniel needs to study harder for English or won't pass the diploma."

"He's got enough learning material," I say.

"That's right, but he needs to study vocabulary. At times he doesn't even understand what we are saying."

"Right, let me talk to him, okay. Is he upstairs?"

"No, he went shopping this morning."

"For what?"

"He says it's personal, and he'll tell you himself."

That morning, young Jimmy went to the doctor. After a preliminary examination, the doctor says: "You seem to be completely healthy. I will need you to have a few more tests done, though, and I'm sure we'll find something."

Jimmy finally reveals the real reason for the doctor's visit. He wanted sterilization.

"Sterilization?" asks the doctor, surprised. "It's an operation that can't be undone. You're 19-years old – you're much too young for something like that."

But Jimmy insists and is professionally sterilized with a complete vasectomy. He was discharged just a few hours after the surgery, and when Jimmy arrived back at home, his mother greeted him eagerly.

"So, have you been in town?"

"Yes, Mom. I went shopping."

"And did you buy something personal?"

"Yes, Mom. I bought a new shirt."

"Very good. And have you been to the doctor?"

"Yes, Mom. I've been to the doctor too."

"And did you get vaccinated?"

"Oh — was I supposed to say vaccination?"

The Red Rag that Followed Me

I'm going to study philosophy because I need the enlightenment, the insights of the centuries.

Yes, time is running out, and I must ascend to another level to save my youth.

After all, I'm already in my mid-twenties. Am I a victim? Probably, maybe not in the traditional sense but a victim nonetheless, because of memories of traumatically embarrassing physical experiences earlier in my life.

You must understand that I was still living with my mother until recently. So, Hotel Mama would be a good term to use.

But everything has an end, except the sausage, which has two, right? So I had just turned 17, and as a favor to someone, I had to move out — simply put, I didn't have a choice. I had to go!

But in all fairness, I did convince someone to pay for a new place to live in the meantime. Talking about fairness, you don't get far without money, and frankly, most people think if you don't have the money, you don't deserve a place to live.

Anyway, surprisingly, my dad agreed to rent a studio for me for six months, conveniently located in the same high rise building my mom lived in.

But there was a catch. I thought the deal with the studio was sealed when my mom arrived with a request.

My mother, a perpetual worrier, said she would agree to the deal only if I accepted her neighbor friend coming over daily to clean the studio. I needed to decide quickly because she, and not my father, would have the final say on my move.

So, I caved. What harm could a cleaner do?

And indeed, I'd barely been in my new pad an hour when I heard a knock at the door. Before I could open it, she walked into the apartment. The old cunt had a key! I asked her about this immediately, but she understood very little English.

While irritating me simultaneously, what caught my attention was the red cleaning rag draped over her shoulder like a sous-chef. She even crawled under the toilet, the furniture, and my bed to ensure everything was cleaned with this red cloth. And every ten minutes or so, she smiled at me and cleared her throat like she needed my attention while I was trying to focus on the computer.

Anyway, over time, it became routine. Gradually, peace came into my home as I got used to her — but not to that damn rag.

Alba, I think her name was, came every day, sometimes around noon but often in the evening. Once, she told me she had several clients, which was odd since my mother said she wasn't getting paid.

More and more, I had the impression that this old hag would follow me everywhere with the red cloth.

On Friday night, I came home, maybe a little drunk after a birthday party, and again, Alba was there — or had she never left?

She was wiping the edge of my bed with that dreaded rag.

"Did you drink too much?" she asked in a heavy accent.

I mumbled something like "stop following me" and immediately got into the shower. I remember the water was lukewarm, and the water pressure sucked.

Suddenly everything became foggy.

My head seemed to be spinning, and somehow, I couldn't help but think of an old ex-girlfriend. She was by far the prettiest girl in high school, without a doubt. I fantasized that we were both in the shower and weren't alone. Anyway, as a man, things began to stir.

It might sound odd, but to be honest, I was excited, right there under the shower. I may have blanked out — I'm not sure, but suddenly I felt a sensation below, and then I saw it. The red rag attached to a wrinkled hand was groping my balls!

Despite the heavy fog in the shower, I could see the rag — and Alba's face. But the most traumatically embarrassing part was her humiliating grin, which I don't think I will ever wipe from memory. I fear what will happen if I ever see a red rag again.

How to Find a Millionaire

My name is Birgit and it all begins tomorrow. Packing the luggage is no cakewalk and although I've been preparing for weeks, I have currently problems to keep a clear head. I need to know what I can take with me and what I have to leave at home.

I'm so excited about the upcoming cruise, especially the huge buffets where I can eat my fill again.

The cruise will start in Italy. It's supposed to be an enormous vessel with several swimming pools and many restaurants. The idea to book a cruise ship vacation came to my mind when I recently met an old friend. She had already spread the news on Facebook that she had finally found her dream man.

Life can be beautiful, winsome and filled with real love, at least that's the idea and hope I still have. The best evidence is my best friend Andrea, because after ten years of online dating she has finally found a handsome boyfriend. And he must be a rich guy, since now I know how much such a cruise trip costs. My trip had cost over five thousand, but her trip *must have been crazy expensive.* My thoughts are wandering between packing and posh guys, cocktails and toiletries. It's better to have plenty of them.

Tampons and shampoos fortunately don't weigh a lot. I hear the doorbell ringing. Who might that be, I have no time!

Hello, Andrea! What a surprise!"

"Hello Birgit, I just wanted to say a last time hello before you start your cruise trip tomorrow. May I introduce you to my fiancé. This is Bobo from Manila."

"I'm pleased to meet you"

"Hi!"

"Does he speak English?"

"He speaks English very well. After all he had worked on the cruise ship where I met him. He's a waiter there …and a very capable man!"

The Hermit

Some people say Michael was a hermit, but that's only partly true.

The truth is, he was originally from the UK, but now he was living isolated in rural Spain near the city of Granada. A hermit, as Michael remembered, is supposed to be poor in material things and he couldn't deny that this was exactly his situation.

He had no electricity and no running water. Sure, he could get some water for cooking as he still had a stove, and in front of his house he had an old generator connected, a "gift" from an old deceased distant neighbor.

Otherwise he was reasonable well equipped. He had a big mattress and a homemade camping toilet.

Once a week he rode on his bicycle to the next village where he went grocery shopping and paid a visit to the local library. Since his arrival he had a dream, he wanted a modern toilet and, even more important, a real, closed panorama window. The problem was, however, that his dwelling had several smaller entrances and at the front a huge, over five metres wide entrance. The entrance was actually opened most of the time because there was no door, no window that'd fit and plastic foil didn't help if it was cold and raining outside.

But the view out of this enormous entrance was fantastic. Michael lived surrounded by mountains and wood on a crest of a hill, from here from here he had a view of all the scenery.

And of course, the view inspired Michael. One day he wanted to become an architect, or maybe an artist and if that didn't work out, he'd still have the option to become the next Ted Kaczynski — or so he thought.

Another problem was that no door and no window would fit into the unusual form of this huge entrance. Friends said that it was impossible to install a panorama window there, because Michael lived in a cave where ten thousand years ago bears and Neandertal people used to live.

A Postcard from Costa Rica

Ms. Graham ordered workers to her house to fix her heating. She lives alone, so she is glad when the men finally arrive around noon. The team consists of only the boss and one apprentice.

Ms. Graham couldn't help but sit on the sofa and watch the men at work as they stood around and discussed the cause and theoretical origin of the damage. If she were a few years younger, she would have flirted with them. But after she thought about it, it was clear that she still had a chance. The tall old man seemed a little sullen, but he was a precise worker nonetheless, although his neatly manicured fingernails didn't quite match his otherwise uncouth appearance. He must be the boss of the troupe, Ms. Graham smiled, an almost devilish idea rising in her head.

She headed towards the kitchen when the men finally began to work. It didn't take them long to find a broken valve. The boss wished to show the broken part to Ms. Graham and explain a few things to her, but she surprised them when she came back with a tray of glasses filled with Tequila. So much for a break.

The men were dumbfounded, at first. "Excuse me ma'am," said the boss, "but we are not allowed to drink on the job."

Ms. Graham pressed the shot glass into his hands. "You haven't even started fixing anything, have you?"

"We were about to."

"And I am about to insist," she said with a smile.

"This isn't very appropriate, ma'am," the youngster commented.

Ms. Grahams eyes widened. "I'll tell you boys what's appropriate here."

The boss looked uncertain, but his face soon softened, and he took the glass from her hand. "Sure, Ms. Graham," he said.

"Absolutely," she replied. "And call me Berta."

"Berta," he said.

She raised the glass. "Gentlemen, before you continue, let's have a toast."

The men showed genuine smiles and raised their glasses as well. "To you, Ms. Graham," the young worker said. "And thanks." They all tipped up their glasses together, gulping down the bitter beverages.

"Better than I thought," the big boss said.

Ms. Graham leaned in very close to him. "I bet I have what you like, darling," she said.

The big boss blushed and wiped his mouth with his hand. He turned to his apprentice. "You know what to do."

The youngster got to work listlessly.

After five minutes, Ms. Graham came back and insisted on another round. The men obeyed and drank. Eventually, the boss ordered the apprentice to head back to the office to get a replacement part.

Over an hour later, the apprentice finally came back to Ms. Graham's house nobody would answer the door. The next day, the boss was nowhere to be found in the office.

Nobody seemed to care too much, since the payments kept coming and the phone remained silent. The apprentice suggested making a missing persons report, but the idea was rejected at once.

"Who cares about old Jack?" The foreman said. "He could be on an extended work trip."

"He could be in China."

"Or stuck in a bar."

The guys laughed.

After about a week, mail arrived at the office; among it was a postcard from the boss from Costa Rica. He let his workers know that he was on a honeymoon with Ms. Graham.

Getting Stoned by Moonlight

I am sitting on the crest of a hill, looking into the dark sky. The moon is almost full, bright and slightly golden, and I think I can make out the Milky Way. It's a clear, cold night. Beautiful, but nothing special.

I came here tonight for a specific reason: I would like to have a spiritual experience on a clear night. I hope for the best, and if it doesn't work out, at least I can say that I tried.

I lean my head back, close my eyes for a moment, and open them as slowly as I can. I hold my index finger in front of my eyes and slowly point my arm towards the moon until my eyes, index finger, and the moon are aligned.

I stay attuned to the moon cycle and the cycle of planets. Now I am aligned with the moon. This is the first step to getting high.

The moon is slowly getting closer to me.

The light is slowly getting brighter.

And, yes, there is light.

And sounds.

At first, it sounds *like very subtle chirping* or squeaking coming from somewhere above, but it slowly comes closer towards the ground, towards me. A little like insects.

I focus on my body and my inner alignment to the moon. I feel I have almost arrived. I feel weightless.

The chirping is now very close, and it is no longer subtle, but rather clear, strange, and loud.

I must keep my eyes closed, but I cannot take it anymore. They are here, creatures around me!

Something is touching my hand, and I want to open my eyes, but I cannot. Now some leathery thing is touching my other hand, and something or someone is holding my feet down. Something very light is touching my private part. I feel as though my body is not sitting on the ground anymore, now certain I am being uplifted.

Silence, darkness.

I am in the state of nonexistence, somewhere between the worlds.

Suddenly, I wake up. I am lying on grass, and it feels cold as ice.

I am confused. I am reaching for my cellphone, but the screen is dark, and I can't get it started.

All around me it is pitch black, the moon and stars gone. Something smells. It is coming from the ground. I touch the grass, but instead of grass, my fingers are stroking through ash. Now I see it: I'm surrounded by a carpet of ash, cold, dark, fluffy ash.

I don't care if they believe me or not; this is all evidence I have been abducted by aliens!

I don't care if anyone believes in the effectiveness of psychedelic mushrooms, but the truth is out there. We are not alone, and huge revelations will be revealed to mankind if we are willing to align with the cycle of the moon.

Cafe Berlin

A German is sitting in a café on Potsdamer Platz in Berlin, relaxing and enjoying a coffee, black bread, and jam breakfast. When, unexpectedly, an American tourist, furiously chewing gum, sits next to him.

Staring at the German's breakfast, he stops snapping his gum long enough to ask, "Do you Germans actually eat all the bread?"

"Yes, of course we do," the German replies.

Loudly bursting the giant gum bubble he just blew, the American says, "We don't. In the States, we only eat the soft part of the bread. We collect the hard crust, form black bread, and send it to Germany."

The German continues to eat undisturbed. But the American asks another question, "Do you also eat jam with your bread?"

"Definitely," The German replies, now slightly annoyed.

The American keeps chewing his gum and says, "We don't. In the States, we only eat fresh fruit for breakfast. So, we collect the peels, seeds, and leftovers in containers, make all sorts of jam and then export to Europe and Germany."

The German, losing interest in the exchange, suddenly has an idea and asks the American, "Do you also have sex in the States?"

"Yes, of course," the American laughs, exposing the stringy gum in his mouth.

"And what do you do with the used condoms?"

The American stops chewing, "We trash them, of course," he says, looking confused.

"Mm, okay, but not us," the German says with an innocent smile. We collect the used condoms in containers, process them into chewing gum, then sell them to America."

It takes a minute, and then it dawns on him. With increasingly horrific realization, the American rushed to spit the gum out.

In his panic and confusion, however, he swallowed it instead.

Uncle Camel

I've been a cigar smoker since Christmas of '96. A small glass of bourbon and a good old Havana helps me to smile about old memories. Here in South Texas, such a break comes in handy on a windy winter day, especially when it's a Sunday afternoon and you're living alone. I remember I still have an uncle in the Texas Panhandle, and when we were young, everybody called him Uncle Camel. Not only was it his nickname, but he truly could drink like a camel.

There is nothing unusual or special about this distant relative. Although he is just an uncle, most people claim we look similar. Although he is a lot older than me, most folks say we look more than alike, that he must be my twin brother or something.

Let me say it openly. We have about half a century of mutual disgust, misunderstanding, jealously, and loads of trouble between us.

I always say, you just do what you can to be a good person. That's why I send him a greeting on WhatsApp every

Christmas, and so far only on Christmas, not on a birthday or anything else.

And honestly, we used to be enemies. He started it by accused me of pocketing his share of the family inheritance, which of course is nonsense. In fact, he's always been weird, a lazy pig, mostly a narcissist. But was I better than him? In hindsight, probably not really.

Here's the story. December 24, 1995. I still lived in Dallas. Back when TV was still in vogue. Anyways, it caught me by surprise seeing his face in the evening news, this round stupid face with a huge mustache was a bank robbery suspect. The story seemed interesting, and it was shown on several different channels, but interestingly, this bank robber was a little different. There was no violence, and according to witnesses, he was polite. The man just went in, kind of shy and stupid, then he left a note for the bank teller that this was a robbery and allegedly told her he carried a gun under his jacket. A real oddball, the commentators said he was smiling all the time.

A day or so later, after the FBI got involved, they caught him. They interviewed him—and now comes the crazy part of the story—the suspect claimed that he was me, that he had my name!

And of course, it didn't take long for them to find me. When they came in here, I was surrounded by at least a dozen agents. Fortunately, I had a picture of Camel and could convince them. Otherwise, I believe I wouldn't be sitting here today.

To make it short, they actually convicted him, and he cried like a baby at the trial.

This all happened a long time ago, but Uncle Camel found God in prison. He better have found the Lord, because only in Him can he find peace.

So, what's the real story? I guess we both have to live with the fact that it was indeed me who robbed that bank back then, up there in the Texas Panhandle.

The Tokyo Fish Market

Today my Japanese friend wanted to show me the highlights for tourists in Tokyo.

Of course, I wanted to see the famous Tsukiji fish market. This market is famous for auctioning tuna, considering some special tuna can reach prices that top $200,000.

We arrived in the early morning and there was already a large crowd of fish traders participating in the auction.

The fish just lay on the floor in various portions. It looked like they had placed a paper slip on all the fishes and caskets; and there was a lot of wild talk at the auction.

I was smiling in awe the whole time, it all looked so interesting and professional. *Somehow I was thinking* Japanese is probably not so difficult to speak; so I said a few words I thought I heard others were saying.

Suddenly I noticed the people started to stare at me and I felt encouraged to say more Japanese words that just popped into my mind. *The stares grew more intense* by the second, and then abruptly my friend took me by the arm, gestured we should go.

We just wanted to leave when somebody said in English that I needed to pay. I didn't understand. My friend then told me, I used the Japanese word for to buy, but I said that it must have been a misunderstanding. Besides I did not have any paper slips.

The Japanese man said, It doesn't matter, my word as a foreigner was good enough to make the purchase.

Boondocking Surprise

Marry seems really upset, but the landscape is beautiful...

"My God, where are we, darling?"

"In the middle of the Rockies, we just left Utah."

"This street looks so strange."

"That's the idea," I say. "We stay off the main road to find a parking spot for the night without being recognized."

"And why all this incognito stuff?"

"It's part of the game, what we call boondocking."

Marry pulls a cigarette out of her pocket and lights it.

"Sweety, no smoking in the car. We talked about that before."

"Yes, when you kidnapped me from the trailer."

"You wanted to come along to know what boondocking is." I remind her.

"You're right, and I wanted to date you too."

"And you're with me all the time now."

"Yeah, in that cluttered van," She mutters, pulling a sour face.

"Also, part of the game," I said, smiling.

"Hey, darling," says Mary. "Do you know where we are? I mean… we're driving down a dirt path in the middle of nowhere."

"There's a small settlement up ahead, I'll ask around."

Sure enough, we find a gas station almost immediately with what looked like a diner attached on the side. Houses are spread out across the wider-valley area, remote to the horizon. The place seems deserted.

"Two guys are standing on the corner." Marry says.

And sure enough, there are two guys right on the roadside, both in white shirts and black pants. I stop and roll down the window. "Sorry," I say, forcing a smile. "Is this the road to Springfield?"

They remained silent, but their faces looked friendly.

"There's supposed to be a Walmart just before Springfield… we're looking for it."

"How are you?" said the smaller of the two. "We would like to ask you something too."

"Sure," I say. "Do you need help?"

"Have you read the Bible?"

"The Bible?" I repeat, wondering if I'd misheard.

Mary leans over. "Yes, we have. Do you know where Walmart is? We must park somewhere tonight."

The man keeps smiling. "The whole Bible —"

"It's okay, folks," I jump in. "We were just asking." I'm about to roll up the window when I hear him say, "wait, we have something for you."

I nod politely and step on the gas pedal. "They were church people," I say.

"Yes, they're usually pretty good folks and very persistent," Marry says.

"I think we just keep on driving. I'm sure we're on the right track." I suggest.

Indeed, as night falls, we arrive at a huge old building with an empty, sprawling parking lot out front.

"Looks like it's closed," says Mary

"Yeah, it looks totally closed, probably shut down for years."

"It looks spooky."

I nod. "Exactly the right place to spend a night undisturbed."

"What about the cops?"

"Here? I don't think so. We're pretty much at the end of the world out here."

Ten minutes later, it's pitch dark, so we prepare for the night as best we can. "Tuna and crackers for dinner." I humbly let her know.

"I feel scared." Marry says.

I keep my mouth shut because, technically, she's right to be. It's lonely and spooky in this massive parking lot.

Somehow sleep is inconceivable.

Marry mumbles something to herself. "I keep hearing something, a noise... I'm not sure what it is," she says.

I found myself feeling slightly jaded. We rolled back and forth on the mattress in the back of the van. "It'll be a short night," I murmur back, trying to comfort her.

Suddenly a blinding light and footsteps.

A knock, then someone's banging on the door.

"My God, the cops are here," screams Marry.

A sharp slice of light shines brightly through the window.

"Just a flashlight. Stay calm." I say.

"We should ask them what they want." Marry suggests, visibly shaken.

I straighten up and open the door a crack.

"Excuse me, sir," a male voice says.

The flashlight shines straight into my face. I shield my eyes with my hand. "What's going on? Can I help you with something?"

"We have something we want to give you," says the voice.

Suddenly I recognize the face behind the light, "You… how? What the hell?"

A hand reaches out to me and presses something bulky into my hand. "Sorry to disturb you, sir, but do you know the Watchtower magazine?"

I recognize the man. It's the guy from the gas station, the churchman.

"Oh my God," Marry gasps, grabbing her face.

"That's right," says the young man. "For us, no road is too long to bring people closer to the Lord — Please read the magazine and have a blessed night."

The Massage Parlor

It all started in Las Vegas, but it didn't stop there. My ex-wife, who I was never married to, actually had a massage license from Florida. However, after my last experience in that industry, I am now rather forced to take an interest in the topic. My online psychiatrist advised intensive, long-term treatment, because after all, I am handicapped. An old motorcycle accident changed the course of my life. The stumps of my legs needed massages.

Anyway, I was recommended a massage salon specializing in leg massages, or so I thought. Frankly, the recommendations came also from compelling billboard ads, and when I asked my ex, all she said was for me to go for it.

That place was a little outside the city—nice villas, all residential—and when I finally walked into their Mansion, I wasn't unimpressed. It was big, though the entrance had tacky white pillars, and everything inside was plush and carpeted. Otherwise, there was no sign of massages or even anything that could be interpreted as medicinal. However, a very friendly staff member asked a very precise question.

She asked whether I needed a so-called Swedish or Norwegian massage style. I couldn't figure. I told her I was only there for the rest of my legs, and an all-body oil massage. I told the ladies about myself, that I am a believer, and that the massage would have to stay clean. I am still a member of the Church, a traditional man, and don't you forget it.

However, it didn't take long when the brunette suggested a beneficial soap massage, just for lowering of my blood pressure, and afterward, an intensive deep-tissue massage for my butt. I said "Fine, let's get it over with!"

After politely refusing personal help in the changing room, I was led to the bathing salon with a towel that was a little too tight around my hips, considering the wheelchair. Anyway, a simple, round hot bath came first. It was more of a Jacuzzi, and when I stumbled into the tub, it wasn't the brunette but a fat Asian lady who had been following me from the toilet, and that creature just kept giggling.

Finally, the secret liquid was let in with a kind of amphora. I just sat in the lukewarm water for a few seconds as a huge foam, like a gigantic cloud enveloping me in bubbling white. Strangely, it smelled more stale like vanilla,

257

similar to an obese person's mouth. And then it all happened so fast. I could hardly see anything, but I felt my lower back massaged first. Pleasant for sure, but the touch was somehow too soft. Finally, it was time for the "medical treatment," the stumps of my legs. Supple hands slowly stroked higher. This went on for several long minutes, and with every second stroke, her hands gradually reached a little higher. To be precise, the hands went up to the inside of my thighs. Oh boy, was that close!

Suddenly, a huge splash. Foam everywhere. Annoyed, I wished it aside, but I couldn't see or feel anything. The whole room was full of foam so thick that I couldn't see my own hands, and there was something big in the water. I called the masseuse, but there was no answer. I guess I was too helpless to get up at that moment, and really didn't care if the girl fell into the water.

I could hardly finish the thought when rough hands began to massage my stomach. But somehow, the massage changed. It wasn't exactly strokes, more like a strange sensation, almost felt like licking. No one was talking, and the hand felt different, almost leathery. Or was it like a rag with a strange texture? But frankly, I was enjoying it. I could tell this was a special massage, all the way. I cannot and will not describe what happened next, somebody might find out my real name, and tell my church…

Anyway, when I had enough and my most private parts hurt from all the unknown ministrations, when I was through with everything, when more relaxing wasn't possible, I took a deep breath and finally tried to move the foam aside.

First, I heard what sounded like mean laugher, then I was dumbfounded.
There, about a yard away, sitting at the fringe, was a chimpanzee, staring at me with his tar black eyes. He opened his mouth and showed me his huge tongue.

Strangers From a Strange World

Even now, Ben Iglesias doesn't know what happened that day. The memory came to him in fragments; a cacophony of sound and vision that didn't quite fit together into a coherent picture. It was like sand between his fingers, trickling away every time he tried to reach for it.

He remembered the flight. It should have been a routine trip, from Mars to Earth, a journey that he had planned extensively, a journey he had already taken four times before. For his crew, it had been their first time piloting a ship, but they'd had simulation experience and were well-prepared. Nothing should have gone wrong.

The moment they had entered Earth's orbit, the system went down. A warning light flickered on at the control panel, and then the alarms had started, blasting through the spacecraft with growing intensity. The atmosphere turned dense, and at some point amid the chaos, Ben had lost consciousness.

When he woke up, everything was silent. The alarms had ceased, and only the thin red strobe of the emergency sign punctuated the air above him.

The bodies of his four crewmates were sprawled around him, unmoving. He knew they were dead. Their eyes were still open, staring blankly at the ceiling of the craft, and their chests were still.

The emergency lights were on, but everything else was dead. There was no static, no alarm, no warnings beeping on the console. Just silence.

He couldn't tell how long had passed since the spacecraft had landed. It must have crashed, judging by the state of chaos around him, debris and equipment toppled over. Somewhere in the rear of the craft, he could hear electricity sparking, and the air was tinged with the smell of burning. He had to get out, before the whole thing went up in flames.

Climbing to his feet, he staggered over to the control panel and took in the readings that were displayed on the cracked monitor. None of them made sense. The weather, the coordinates, even the time and date… none of it could be correct. The readings must have gone haywire when the system malfunctioned. He pressed the button on the comms system, trying to reach base, but it was dead. Everything was dead.

When he glanced out of the spacecraft's narrow windows, he struggled to understand what he was seeing. He should have been somewhere on the shore, near La Havana Cuba. They'd come down just over the Caribbean Sea. But instead, the landscape stretched on in shades of yellow and brown

Ignoring the pain in his head, Ben eventually exited the spacecraft, leaving behind the bodies of his crew, and stepped out onto the white sand. The desert seemed to roll on forever, towards a burning sun that made mirages on the horizon. The atmosphere was stifling, and according to his tech, there was only 60% oxygen present. He could feel his chest tightening up, but forced himself to take slow, calm breaths. Panicking would only make it worse.

Where was he?

All he could see, for miles around, was that glinting golden sea of sand. No buildings or man-made structures, just dunes and peaks and a few rocks in the distance.

He was in the middle of nowhere. The supplies he had on the spaceship were likely trapped beneath the debris, and he didn't know how long he had before the craft went up in flames. He had to get away from it, but where would he go?

There was nowhere *to* go but forward, towards the burning sun.

The air here was sweltering and sweat beaded along his brow as he slipped over the sand in his space suit. He'd have to take it off sooner or later, but for now, he'd rather keep it on, if only for the extra layer of protection it afforded.

He kept walking, the sands shifting constantly underfoot as the sun bore down on him, until his body gave in to exhaustion. The crash had already weakened him, and when he glanced back, he realized he'd barely made it more than a few meters away from the ship itself.

Sinking to his knees in the sand, Ben closed his eyes. How had this happened? What had caused the ship's system to fail, bringing them down to Earth hundreds of miles off course? It didn't make sense to him. His crew was dead, and he was all alone. He doubted he would last much longer in this heat anyway, not without food or water. A sense of complete hopelessness descended on him, and he began to shake. Why had this happened to him? What had he done to deserve such a horrible twist of fate?

Wind buffeted the side of his face, blowing sand against his eyelids. He couldn't stay here. He had to keep moving. Even if it hurt, he couldn't just give up.

When his eyes flickered back open, he realized he was not alone. Cresting the peak of a nearby sand dune was a figure.

Ben reached up vigorously to rub his eyes, thinking he was hallucinating, but then more of them appeared, small dark shadows blotting the horizon.

People. There were *people*.

Ben tried to climb to his feet, but his knees buckled again, and he landed hard in the sand.

The first figure began shuffling down the dune towards him, and he stayed where he was. From what he could see, they did not carry weapons, and seemed more curious than aggressive.

They were like no people he had ever seen before, but he didn't know what else they could be. They had the same build and features of humans, but they were also much shorter.

As the group of people reached him, they clustered around him in a semi-circle staring down at him. But even on his knees, Ben was almost as tall as they were standing up.

There were mostly women present, and a couple of men, but their skin was dark and painted with chalk, different to his pale skin and light hair. Their eyes, too, were unusual. Like dark stones, set deep into their faces. One woman in particular caught his eye; her eyes were black and shining, almost like a cat's. She cocked her head slightly when she realised he was looking at her.

Who were these people? Were they Australian Aborigines? There was some resemblance, but they were smaller and thinner, almost skeletal in appearance, and their skin was rough like the sand.

The man in front of him pulled a water skin from the string around his waist and offered it to Ben. When Ben hesitated, he gestured for him to drink, tipping the skin towards him.

Ben finally nodded, taking the water from him with trembling, sand-burned hands. He took a sip, feeling the cold liquid wash down his throat, and then another, careful not to take too much.

"Thank you," he rasped, handing the water back to the man.

The stranger then motioned for Ben to follow. Two of the women came forward to help Ben to his feet, one of them being the woman with the cat-like eyes, who was at least four heads shorter than him. Despite their small bodies, they had surprising strength, and managed to get him to his feet with minimal effort.

The man gestured again for Ben to follow, so he did. It wasn't like he had anywhere else to go. Only forward.

The mysterious people led him through the desert, over the dunes and peaks, until they came to the valley of stones that Ben had seen in the distance. When he glanced back, his spacecraft was nothing but a smudge on the horizon.

The rocks here were white, sun-bleached, and covered with small holes. The woman with dark eyes tapped the stone with her finger, white chalk smearing onto her skin, and gestured for him to look inside.

He complied, stepping up to a hole that was big enough for him to squeeze through.

Inside was a cave system with a high-arching ceiling, stalactites hanging down like teeth. From deeper inside, he could hear water striking stone. The rocks must soak up moisture and deposit it deep in the system.

He looked in amazement at the woman next to him, and her lips curved into a faint smile. Ben found himself smiling back.

Someone shouted behind him, a word he did not recognize, in a language he did not know, and he turned.

The man from before was standing before him, holding out a strange looking fruit. He mimicked eating it, before holding it out to Ben. He took it with a grateful nod, sinking his teeth into the soft flesh. The fruit was like nothing he had tasted before, filling his mouth with a sweet, tangy aroma. With food and water in his stomach, he could feel his strength returning. He was saved, after all. He owed his life to these people. But now more than ever, he realized he was stuck here. These people lived in the desert, lived off the land. They had no infrastructure, no supplies. Just the remnants of a civilization. Surely that meant there was nothing here.

Nowhere to go, no method of travel but to walk across the sands.

He was still alone. He could not speak with these people, did not know their language, their customs. He was a stranger here.

Once he had finished the fruit, licking the juices from his fingers, he tried to thank the people around him. He got to his knees and pressed his head to the dusty rocks, trying to communicate his gratitude for saving him.

A hand gently touched his shoulder, and when he looked up, he was staring into those beautiful black eyes again. The woman shook her head gently, signaling for him to stand, so he did.

"Thank you," he said again, unsure if they could understand him. "My name is *Ben*." He pointed to himself, repeating his name.

"Ben," the people around him repeated.

The man pointed to himself next and said in a slow voice: "Ruma."

"Ruma," Ben repeated, nodding, then turned to the woman expectantly. She seemed surprised to be asked, but also gestured to herself.

"Lera."

"Lera," he said softly. "Lera."

The woman seemed to grow sheepish, taking a step back, and Ben smiled in amusement. Perhaps they weren't so strange after all.

That night, Ben lay under the stars, cushioned by the rocks in the valley. He could not sleep. His thoughts would not settle, going round and round in his head like a sputtering engine.

What now?

He had been saved by these people, given food and water and shelter, but what came next? His ship was broken, his crew was dead. Nobody knew where he was; nobody would come looking for him. He could hardly even tell how long had passed since he was last at the space station. The journey between Mars and Earth already seemed so long ago. It felt as though time had already changed, propelling him into a future he wasn't expecting. The world here was not the world he remembered, but different. Like he had been away for many more years than he knew.

Perhaps he had. Time could be a fickle thing in space. And the crash, landing amid this unknown land, the coordinates and temperature, everything that had been displayed on the ship's control panel – everything he thought was incorrect – might not be so far-fetched after all. If their entry into the Earth's orbit had torn through time itself, things would begin to make a lot more sense.

But Ben couldn't be sure. He couldn't communicate with these people, couldn't ask them the year or the day, if they even had the same calendar he was familiar with.

There was no point in pondering things he could not know. It would only drive him mad.

Instead, he should focus on the rational dangers ahead of him. Like the fact that he was trapped here, in the golden sands of some unknown land, without any means of getting back home.

The hopelessness of his situation came crashing back down to him, leaving him gasping for air.

He got up, shaking the dust from his clothes, and went to the edge of the stony ridge, looking out across the darkness. The stars shone brighter here than he had ever seen, creating a silver mist along the horizon.

A figure stepped up beside him, silent as a cat.

"Lera," he whispered.

She said something in her tongue, and he looked at her. She was pointing up to the sky. She said it again, and he realized she was telling him the word for the stars. He repeated it, looking up at where he'd come from. He'd come from the stars. A place as mysterious and unknown as this. But a place he had once called home.

"Home," he said out loud, and Lera repeated it in her gentle voice.

"This is your home?" Ben continued, gesturing around him.

Lera squinted, trying to gauge the meaning of his words, before nodding.

She pointed to the rocks, and then the sand, saying each word slowly so that he could repeat it after her.

The night passed like this, the two of them sitting on the rocks while Lera tried to teach him her language.

After a few days, Ben was starting to get the basics. With nowhere else to go, he'd decided to stay. These people had no qualms about taking him in, and they provided him food and water from their stores, and in return, he used his stronger body to help them shift rocks and collect water from inside the caves.

A week passed, and then another.

Ben began to change. He grew accustomed to a life among the rocks and the sand. His skin began to turn golden, taking on the same rough, sandy texture as the sand dwellers. He grew more confident in their language, achieving basic communication, thanks to Lera's instruction.

There were still moments where, in the silence and the solitude, he'd feel a sense of displacement, like he didn't really belong here. And the memories of the crash, the mystery of what had happened, still haunted him. He would have nightmares of what happened, waking up in the dead of night in a panic, mourning his dead crew, his vulnerability.

But then Lera would be there, soothing him with her gentle voice, stroking her delicate fingers through his hair.

He grew closer to her over those weeks, almost never straying from her side. They collected water together, travelled across the sands together, to the only trees that bore fruit for miles around. She was the community's healer too, and she taught him how to make medicines from the plants that grew there, crushing them into pastes that healed the sores and scrapes they sustained from living in such a harsh environment.

He began to forget his past, who he used to be. He forgot what it was like to travel among the stars, ferrying his ship from one planet to the other. He remembered what it was like to live *beneath* the stars, to feel small and insignificant under a vast sky. The mystery of what happened that day faded with dawn.

His nightmares faded. He was no longer plagued by the desire to know the truth, to know what had happened to his spacecraft and his crew, to know why his ship had crashed without reason. It didn't matter anymore. That part of his life was over now, buried in the sand.

This was his new life, here in this strange new world, with these strange new people.

He had a home here, a new calling, and a woman who he had begun to love.

The troubles of his past did not bother him here. So here he would stay.

Working Shoes

The fact is, I am well into middle age, and evidently, I feel that my sexual life hasn't been fulfilling.

I was married before I turned twenty-one, and truthfully, after thirty-five long years, not much of a sexual life exists.

Yes, I am still married to Barbara. Kids? That would have been impossible. You see, you cannot suck water out of a stone, as we say here in Disneyland, where we live close by.

Yet, I never complained about it. I don't discuss it much, and neither does Barbara. But I know she talks to her chubby best friend about these things, and I am not bitter; these are the facts.

For instance, the other day, the three of us were walking around the mall when she casually and, too loudly, told her friend, "Back in 1982, on Christmas day, I touched Al, and it felt awkward."

I am telling you this because we had just walked into the same mall we've always shopped at since we were 21 — but no, I'm not frustrated, just musing at the facts.

After all, which middle-aged man wouldn't go shopping with his wife on their day off, right?

"Are you okay?" Barbara's voice instantly brought me back to reality.

"All good, nothing new."

She steps in front of me and looks me straight in the eyes. "Al, you look confused. Did you take your meds?"

"Of course... always."

Her face darkened. "No, *not* like always, and don't pretend you don't know what I mean, Al."

I shook my head. "I'm serious. I really don't know what you mean. But, please, let's not make a scene here."

"Al, listen to me," now she pointed her finger at me, "when you are confused, you become irrational, and you know it."

"Irrational?"

"Yes, you confuse numbers and other simple regular things."

"Babs, I'm okay, really."

"I hope so. Promise me to take your pills as soon as we get home."

"I promise," I say sheepishly. "What are we doing here?"

"We are here to buy shoes, Al, don't you remember?"

I smiled: "Ah yes, you got that right."

"Because you need strong shoes for the garden, remember?"

"Now I do. Solid shoes, and the right size, of course."

And then, there it was — the last shoe shop in the mall, and most importantly, Babs' favorite one.

"But let me do the talking," I said, feeling moderately confident.

"The floor is all yours," she said graciously. "I will not even look in your direction."

"Excuse me, do you sell working shoes?" I ask the salesperson, a young girl dressed unusually conservatively.

The girl said they had a special-price sale on work shoes. Just then, I was drawn to a particularly sturdy-looking pair on the shelf, so I asked if they kept my size.

"Sorry," she replied, "those are the only ones, and there are no guarantees on any shoes on sale."

"What a bargain," I said when I saw the price, and I bought the shoes for the next day's gardening.

Babs and I walked home very content with ourselves. Considering I made it through the day without my medication, it was a productive and pleasant afternoon. And that's a fact.

The following morning I'm wearing my new shoes in the garden, trying to get used to them, but something doesn't feel right.

I tell Babs that I am not complaining but need to return to the mall right away and explain later.

It took much longer than I thought, and it was evening when I returned home, limping from my "wounded" heel.

Babs shakes her head. "Why did you have to buy shoes that don't fit, Al?"

"Only the one shoe is too small, Babs — that's why they were such a bargain."

Equity Crowdfunding

For years, I had been planning to acquire a new kitchen. The problem was that I was still living at my parents' home, more specifically, in the attic.

Sometimes I didn't even know if I really was in a completely bleak situation or if I just needed to start looking at things from a different perspective. Just recently, I tried it at a bank, and how they laughed when I pitched my request for a loan for a new kitchen. And yes, I had to laugh along, because it just came out that way.

It was kind of funny too. Still living with your parents over 30, unmarried and with almost no income, and above all still without your own kitchen, is odd. I always tell myself life gives, life takes.

And yet, a new kitchen was needed, one way or the other.

"Daddy, do you have a minute?"

He didn't even look up as he sat down with his breakfast omelet. "Go ahead," he said.

"I can't cook upstairs anymore."

"Then serve yourself from our kitchen."

I stopped in the doorway. He already knew. "I need money for a new kitchen."

"What's wrong with the old one?"

"Dad, what I have upstairs is not a real kitchen, you know that."

He kept silent for a moment, then looked up. "We don't have that kind of money."

"I know," I said.

"Well, then, get an income."

And that was it. I cried for most of the rest of the day.

But the fact was, I had a tiny, outdated kitchenette, like in a hotel, equipped with a microwave oven and an electric water kettle. It didn't even fit in with my room, and it didn't fit to my interests. See, I loved to rummage in cookbooks and had already downloaded hundreds of recipes, and to be honest, I think I am a pretty decent cook. And yes, I am still waiting for a husband to show him all of my skills, but who cares, right?

And by the way, my parents, to this day, eat all that crappy plain food, like fries, beans, sausages, and other coarse ingredients.

I am not the only one with high expectations. My mom expressed more than a few times that I should finally find a partner, get married, and so on. But there was a problem.

Unemployment makes life difficult. Still, with or without work, I needed a new kitchen.

I remember I had saved about six hundred dollars, and so I knew I needed some sort of funding. But even with over a thousand online followers, it would take years to gather five thousand bucks.

Although I am from a small town, around the corner we have this big home center that had discounts for kitchens on Mondays. Hardware stores, just like supermarkets, can be places where you sometimes see neighbors and friends.

So on a Monday morning around Christmas time, I found myself standing in front of the main entrance, just waiting. Then, after twenty minutes, an old neighbor came, and I didn't hesitate for a second.

"Excuse me ma'am," I said with an odd smile.

The old lady stopped. "Yes?"

"Do you have some change?"

"Oh, it's you. How are you?"

"Well, I am in a little bit of a situation."

Her face darkened a little. "Are you panhandling here?"

I pressed my lips together and exhaled. "My pressure cooker broke down, and I need some money to get a new one."

She stopped right in front of my face. "A cooker?"

"Yeah," I tried to smile. "I'm only 30 dollars short."

"I think they sell kitchen appliances," she answered.

"Yes, they do, and I need help buying one."

"Thirty dollars?"

"Anything would help," I said innocently.

She paused for a moment, then pulled her wallet out of her handbag. She looked at the bill and handed me a 20 dollar note.

"Ma'am, I'm very grateful."

She nodded and moved on.

And that was it, it really worked. So a bit later, I met half a dozen people I had seen somewhere before, and most gave me something. A few started conversations, but in the end, I accepted all I could get, and by midday, I had enough money for an in-house down payment on a Miele kitchen.

When I came home my dad asked: "Where have you been?"

"Crowdfunding," I said proudly.

A Monk's Measure

Since quitting a certain habit, I am trying to live a happier life. A good start was changing my location, so currently I am travelling from the north to the very south of Japan. I found a beautiful park in the ancient city of Kyoto; my mind started wandering. Not far away, I saw a large antique temple, about three stories high and all in rusty red. I had no idea what this structure meant or why it stood there.

Anyway, I was quite curious about it because I heard Japanese temples are supposed to be different.

When I stretched my neck to see the rooftop, I felt somebody was watching me

I turned around. Not even three feet behind me stood this diminutive Japanese monk.

"Christ, what the hell", I mumbled.

He stared at me and said, "Jesus was probably a Buddhist monk."

I took a step back. "Right. And I'm the pope."

He smiled. "Historical research proved it. Don't you want to learn something?"

"Maybe", I said. "But I agree, spirituality is interesting."

"There is a reason for everything."

"Is that really true, boy?"

"Look around, stranger, behind you is a temple and in front of you a Buddhist."

"Sorry, but that doesn't mean anything."

"Let me explain it to you".

I shook my head. "It's not necessary. I have to go now."

I took a few steps back, but the monk moved closer at once.

"Are you following me?"

He smiled. "You first said you wished to learn something about spirituality, as you call it."

"I already did, thank you."

"Remember, you are not as important as you might think, stranger."

I got a bit agitated. "What do you mean?"

"You are a nobody!"

I took a deep breath. "I think I've had enough of you, now beat it!"

"Don't you still want to learn something?"

"Yeah, of course I do", I said as I spat on the ground.

"Good, then say aloud, I am nothing,"

I refused. Now I'd really had enough of this clown.

"You are a damn fool; you really want me to believe that Jesus was a Buddhist, fuck off!"

"I'm giving you a free lesson in Buddhism..."

I interrupted. "You are not a monk, you are a fake, a fucking tourist trap, now get out of my face!"

And jeez, did I insult him, he got the whole package! But when I'd said my piece, the monk quietly asked, "If someone offers you a gift, and you refuse to accept it, does that make the gift yours or the one who offered it?"

"It belongs to the one who offered it, now fuck off!"

"In the same way," replied the monk, "The words with which you have insulted me are all yours."

I walked away, sniffing on my little bottle, inhaled something....., and felt better instantly, although a bit foggy. Suddenly there was a light in front of my eyes, and then it made all sense! I got enlightened!

The Au Pair

The French parents of Nicole meant well with their daughter. They wanted to send her daughter as an au pair to England to learn English. An agency had organized accommodations for Nicole with an English family.

The agency had charged the parents a lot of money for a one month stay; but it didn't matter since their daughter's education was most important. Nicole was excited because she had never been out of the county before; and she would love to learn a new language.

It was August when Nicole finally traveled to England. However, when Nicole arrived she was in for a nasty surprise. She was not allowed to make phone calls and there was no internet. Therefore, Nicole had to go the post office to send her parents letters the old fashion way. In the end, Nicole had returned to France before the parents could receive them. However, they were all very happy to see their daughter again and of course they wanted to know if Nicole *could speak fluent English, after* all.

The daughter explained: "No, I have not learned English since the host family spoke more Hindu than English. They were immigrants from India."

"This means that the whole trip was in vain," the mother lamented.

"No, not at all," Nicole replied. "I now know what Masala fish is."

He Won the Jackpot

I was sitting in my bar, which is not that unusual since I consider myself an afternoon drinker. Then, suddenly, the door opened, and my nephew and his friend hurriedly approached me.

"You're not going to believe it," my nephew says, trying to impress me.

"What is it," I say.

"Uncle Larry won the jackpot!"

I shake my head, unimpressed. "Nah, he doesn't even win a beer at Bennigans."

"I swear!" The boy points to his goofy friend, who seems to be freezing. "This is Mickey, Uncle Larry's stepson."

I give him a friendly nod. "Hey kid, how's it going?"

"Just fine, Mr. Jones."

"Call me Jimmy, so your dad won, huh? What did he play?"

"The Powerball."

"Nice," I try to smile. "So he won big, like what, six numbers?"

The boy shrugs. "I suppose he did. I heard he bought himself a yacht."

"Is that right? How do you know that?"

"An asset broker came to our house, wanted to talk to my dad. That's how I found out."

"Hey T," my nephew says. "I can go down to Fort Lauderdale and check things out."

I thought for a second. "You know what. We'll go together."

"That's great, T."

"Let's find this motherfucker. Your uncle owes me."

A minute later, we all hop into my Ram. On the way, I explain to the boys that Uncle Larry owes 100 grand worth of debt to our family.

We arrive just before midnight. The old shotgun house looked unchanged outside, with stray dogs and garbage everywhere.

"I bet he's hiding the stash someplace near that dumpster," I remark.

"How are we going to handle him?" my nephew asks.

"We always start by being polite," I say.

"And what if he doesn't want to pay?"

"We keep being polite until it's time not to be."

"Look, his car is still there. So, he must be in the house."

"That ain't his car," I say, squinting and pointing my finger at the strange old vehicle in the dark.

"I think he's got something."

"Like what?" I ask.

"It's too dark, but it looks like an old-timer, a classic."

"He always had peculiar tastes," I say.

We don't want to waste any more time and decide to pay him a visit right away. As he opens the door, the smell of crusty old beer mugs hits us.

At first, he tries to argue but then confesses that he never won the lottery. He had bragged that he did, just to show off. I am not convinced. I demand my money either way. Finally, after a heated exchange, he gave me the car keys. The car did little to put a dent in the debts, however. I continued to glare at him. Then, very slowly, he handed me his lottery ticket to check if it was worth anything. As it turned out, it was typical uncle Larry — big sinner, no winner.

The Three of Us in Paris

Love is a serious mental disease

-Plato

In a café in Paris, I sit at a table with my best friend Judy. Across from us sits Pierre, smiling at me. I met Pierre on my first trip to France three years ago. He helped show me around the city after I got lost one day, and we have kept in touch ever since.

Pierre is holding my hand, but I am still shaken.

"So, your husband let you go to Paris by yourself?" He asks.

"Yes," I say. "He said he had some urgent business in Brooklyn.".

Pierre shakes his head.

Judy sips her smoothie, then shakes her head too. She isn't convinced. "I don't understand. What happened over the last few days?"

"Well, it's complicated," I say.

"C'mon! Why don't you tell us what's happened?"

I start to explain it from the beginning, or I try, at least. "My husband, as you know, is very busy with his business, and he is part of a larger group, so to speak."

Pierre seems unable to stop his grin. "You never told me."

"Forget it, honey."

"Tell me," he insists. "What does your husband do?"

I cough into my fist. "My husband owns a private spa. With a pool, massages, all of that stuff."

"That's great. You love happy endings?"

"No," I say. "In the States, it is very different. It's all legit there."

Pierre winks at me, smiling like the devil.

"Well, Jonny and I had some issues," I admit.

"Like what?"

"I am convinced to this day that he cheated on me with one of the masseuses. I needed a break, so I asked Judy to join me on this trip."

"And you have not regretted it, Am I right, my love?

"No, of course not."

We finish the overpriced *la-fettes*, then Judy and I go back to our semi-luxurious hotel, a converted old apartment with no elevator or lamps to speak of. Before we arrive, we decide to make a detour to one of the amazing bridges over the river.

It looks all very picturesque. Directly under us flows the Seine River, and the beauty of the gilded statues and all of the fancy metal fences take us by surprise.

"Oh my God, who built all of this?" Asks Judy.

"Their king had a lot of money."

"Gosh, I wish we had something like that in the States."

I nod. "Yeah, but I read that their king just died recently."

Suddenly, the phone rings. "It's Jonny!"
When I answer, a cranky voice speaks. "So, how's everything in Paris?"

"Hi Jonny, I wish you could see everything! It's incomparable!"

"How is the French toast?"

"They call it something different here. *Orovoa*, I think."

"Alright, take good care of yourself." Jonny hangs up.

Judy shakes her head. "He is always calling at odd hours, isn't he?"

"I did tell him that there is a time difference, you know."

Later that evening, we wait in front of a traditional Parisian restaurant with exceptional garlic bread and pasta. We wait and chat, but after 15 Minutes, Pierre still hasn't shown up.

"He isn't coming" Judy says.

"Unreliable, the men here. Still care about the restaurant?"

She shakes her head. "It would cost us hundreds."

We leave, and after getting lost for a little, we finally we find a Tony Roma's. "Halleluja", I shout in excitement.

But this restaurant felt different, for some reason I could not focus on the not so original food, because I had to think back to the night Pierre and I got together, the wonderful conversations we had, how quickly we got to know one another. I hold my coffee cup tight.

Judy looks at me with a long pause, *observing me.*

"Where did you guys meet again?"

"On my first trip here, three years ago. Jonny was stuck in the hotel room with stomach cramps."

"I bet you went out more than once-"

I interrupt with a wave of my hand. "I know, but then I had already met Pierre. He's a wonderful tour guide. He showed me around the entire city."

"Really?"

"Really. I think I'm going to invite Pierre to the States to return the favor."

And so it happens. One year later, we are sitting in a café together once again, this time a Starbucks somewhere in Jersey. Me, Judy, and Pierre, who hasn't aged a day. He still looks just as handsome as the day we met.

I smile, touching Pierre's knee. "Pierre, why don't you tell Judy what happened last night?"

Pierre leans back, smiles. "Okay, let me tell the story from my perspective…"

Judy leans forward in her seat. "Details, please."

"Well, we were in the middle of our act, right in my bedroom, as Jonny was supposed to be on a short business trip, when I suddenly heard the rattle of a key coming from the front door."

"And now comes the best part," Pierre adds.

I remember I said: "Get out, get out quick, my husband is coming!"

"And so I did." Pierre says.

"I said, take the backdoor Pierre!"

Pierre smiles wistfully. "But I was surprised that I had to cut my pleasure short, darling"

"What do you mean Pierre?" Judy asks.

"Well, looking back I have to say, having all the fun from the doggy style position, I should have stayed no matter what."

North of the Border

I was in an irritated sort of mood. "Last night, we talked about marriage and what it would mean for us, right?" I said, turning to look at Jenny.

Jenny slipped on her lipstick and glanced in the rear-view mirror before pursing her lips several times. "We did, and it was nice."

"Was it?" I said dryly. "Then why were you messing around on Tinder this morning?"

Jenny stared at her exposed teeth. "Oh please, that's nothing. I was about to delete my profile."

"Glad to hear it, because we're about to go on a special vacation, remember?"

"I know...a road trip to Mexico by car."

"It's an American-built truck," I pointed out.

"Ok, nice to know."

At that moment, we approached a curve, and what we saw next took our breath away.

"Oh my gosh, what's happening?" Jenny looked shocked as a line of cars and trucks appeared as far as the eye could see.

I shook my head. "We're nearing the border."

"No, look! The entire road up ahead is lined with pickup trucks!"

I glanced at her. "And looking at your face, I can tell that's the worst pickup line you've ever *seen*."

Shortly before the border, I heard a thump as I caught a glimpse of a shadow across the rearview mirror. Someone had jumped into the truck's bed —

I stopped immediately and went to look. I spot a strange, older man huddled anxiously in a corner. "What are you doing in my truck?" I asked.

For seconds he just stared at me. And then, in a raspy voice, "I must reach Mexico."

"Yeah? You can walk to the border. Why did you jump in my truck?"

"Sir, please... I beg you. I am not a criminal. I just don't have a passport."

I shake my head. "You have drugs on you or something?"

"No, I am an artist."

"Listen, man," I said. "Even if I let you stay, the border patrol will catch you with half a look."

297

"I can hide under a tarp."

"I'm sorry, a what?"

He pulled what looked like a dirty canvas out of a duffle bag.

"This is a canvas from an oil painting," he explained. "I'll hide under it...it'll work."

Jenny got curious and stared at the stranger like her eyes would pop out any second. "Sammy," she said, looking worried. "You're not seriously considering giving this bum a ride, are you?"

"He's an artist; he needs some help."

"So?"

"Well, we claim to be artists, remember?"

Jenny tilts her head spitefully. "Are you saying we have to help each other?"

I looked at his canvas. "You're not a Jackson Pollock or someone famous, right?"

He grinned, then shook his head.

"If we get through, you give me your painting?" I asked expectantly.

"Whatever it takes," he said. "But I prefer to paint you a new one."

I nodded, half smiling. "Okay, but you better start right away."

"You got it, boss," he said.

Jenny looked at me, slightly confused: "So, what do you call a guy that paints in the back of a truck?"

"… I'd call him a pickup artist," I said, deadpan.

The Gas Station

Based on a True Story

I wasn't intoxicated in any way, but I stumbled out of the car. With 65 I feel too young for retirement, but am not a spring chicken anymore, I smiled. For a second, I pondered whether I should go to the toilet first or start pumping gas. Why was I so confused?

Somehow, I managed to push the pump into the tank hole. "Wait," I said loudly, fumbling in my pocket and pulling out my wallet. My suspicions were confirmed immediately. I had exactly one dollar left. The tank was empty, and there was no doubt I would get stuck up on I-95. I would definitely have been questioned by a cop without manners.

"Nah," I spat, and with a very gentle two-fingered squeeze, I began to pump the gas in spurts. 30 cents... 85 cents... a little more... 105. Shoot! Was that too much? I look around, but everything looked blurry. I took a deep breath.

"Let's get out of here," I murmured.

I jumped into my car, turned the ignition key, and hit the pedal. It jerked. *Damn the engine if it lets me down now*, I thought. I accelerated again.

There were screams coming from somewhere. The world had gone mad. I stepped on the gas again. Why wouldn't the car move?

A bang, someone kicked my car. *Not with me asshole.* The second I opened the car door, I couldn't believe my own eyes. Gasoline spurted out of the pump like a broken fire hydrant. Shadows were running in all directions, then it dawned to me. Shoot! In fact, I forgot to take the pump out of the car, and the hose had burst!

What should I do? Suddenly the gas stopped flowing, and I pulled out the broken tube out and took it to the shop. I would explain. As soon as I was inside, I realized I had made a mistake. The guy at the register was 7 feet tall at least, fat like an elephant, and had disgusting scars on every patch of his skin. I was about to ask if he had syphilis or something when the fat man yelled: "Get the fuck outa here before the cops come."

"I only have a dollar," I replied. He stared at me in disbelief. "I have you covered. Now beat it, before somebody gets hurt!"

Of course, I left at once. Luckily, I did not get stuck due to my lack of gas, and I actually made it home. But this is not the end of the story.

Later that night, just a minute before I reached my home, I actually got stopped by a patrol car, and it happened really fast. But it wasn't for the incident at the gas station. The cop accused me that I was driving on the wrong side of the road without a seatbelt.

***

Milton Keynes UK
Ingram Content Group UK Ltd.
UKHW020908170524
442682UK00007B/70